Thomas Herbert Noyes

Lyrics and Bucolics

The Eclogues of Virgil, a Selection from the Odes of Horace, and...

Thomas Herbert Noyes

Lyrics and Bucolics
The Eclogues of Virgil, a Selection from the Odes of Horace, and...

ISBN/EAN: 9783744773317

Printed in Europe, USA, Canada, Australia, Japan

Cover: Foto ©Andreas Hilbeck / pixelio.de

More available books at **www.hansebooks.com**

LYRICS AND BUCOLICS.

THE ECLOGUES OF VIRGIL,

A SELECTION FROM THE ODES OF HORACE,

AND

THE LEGEND OF THE SIBYLL.

TRANSLATED

By T. HERBERT NOYES, Junr.

LONDON:
PUBLISHED FOR THE AUTHOR.
JOHN CAMDEN HOTTEN, PICCADILLY.
1868.

WYMAN AND SONS,

ORIENTAL, CLASSICAL, AND GENERAL PRINTERS,

GREAT QUEEN STREET, W.C.

DEDICATION.

———o———

Virgil to Varus once inscribed his lays,
    And deem'd the' illustrious name would lustre lend
To his sweet strains, which needed no such glaze ;
    Now Varus lives by virtue of his friend :
Friendship still lingers in our later days—
    On whom shall I my little dole expend ?

Unknown to fame, to fortune quite unknown—
    The Dame I mean—her daughter knows me well !
I scarce dare hope, that all the wit I own,
    Will win for me one whiff of Maro's spell,
Or set me on a footstool by his throne.

Then why should I engraft upon my page
    The name I fain would honor, if my lays
Will lift it to no dais on the stage ?
    I'll pay no honest debts with worthless praise.

Then should I rather take some titled name,
　　And dub it for the nonce " my noble friend,"—
The royal road to cheap and spurious fame,—
　　And flaunt whatever lustre that can lend !

So let the ruck : No borrowed plumes for me,—
　　I'll don my own, or else put up with none :
I scoff at no time-honoured pedigree,
　　But tinsel gauds, that glitter in the sun,

I spurn them all.　Content to bide my time,
　　I'll grasp the thorns, and trust to find the rose :
I will not give my friends untested rhyme :
　　I'll dedicate this venture to my foes.

CONTENTS.

———o———

THE LEGEND OF THE SIBYLL.

THE EPILOGUE.

PREFACE.

———o———

IT seems superfluous to explain to my readers that the term " Bucolics," usually but incorrectly translated " Pastorals," means simply the " Lays of the Ox-herds."

The term " Eclogue," by which the several lays are generally known, means nothing more than "Selections," and answers to the term " Idylls," used by Theocritus, whom Virgil imitated in these poems. They are said to have been begun by the poet at the age of twenty-nine, and to have been completed in three years, A.U.C. 713–716. Their publication created no small sensation at Rome. and it was their beauty which induced Mecænas to propose to the poet to follow them up with the Georgics, which were not completed till his forty-fifth year, and not till then was the Æneid begun. I do not propose to enlarge upon the life of Virgil in introducing these, his earliest lays, in a new dress to an English audience.

My classical readers will know already all that I could tell them; and if I should be so fortunate as to interest any whose studies have led them to browse exclusively in other than classic pastures, they will be at no loss where to turn for the missing lore. But I am told that the event is unlikely, for that in these practical days poetry has lost its ancient hold on the imaginations of men—that the writers of fiction stand now where poets stood of yore, and that of the very small portion of popular favour still bestowed on rhymes, pastorals enjoy the smallest fraction, and are least in unison with the spirit of the age. It may be so. We are doubtless a great deal wiser than our ancestors, and little in the habit of echoing the sentiments of Virgil's friend,—

> Ætas parentum, pejor avis, tulit
> Nos nequiores :

And perhaps the old Romans, who applauded the lays of the ox-herds, were quite in the wrong. But I will not think so. To paraphrase what an eminent philosopher has said with regard to the study of metaphysics :— " Whatever nation has given up poetry is in a state of intellectual insolvency. Though its granaries should be bursting, its territories netted with railroads, its mills and founderies the busiest in

the world, the mark of the beast is on it, and it is
going the way of all brutality." Well, I am slow to
believe that we have embarked on that voyage. I
am inclined to think that it is the fault of modern
poets, rather than their readers, if much modern
poetry does not gain a hearing nowadays. It is
either too abstruse, and requires too much thought
and study to take a swift hold of the imagination ;
or the beauty of the shell, maybe, is not sufficiently
attractive to make up for the emptiness of the kernel.
And the attempt to transplant the acknowledged
gems of other languages into our own, is too often
marred by a servile adherence to the letter ; the
result being that the poet is made to speak with a
foreign accent, which is an insuperable drawback to
his popularity. No two languages, that I know of,
admit of a literal interchange of ideas, or precise
identity of phraseology ; and I hold that whoever
sacrifices the idiom of his mother tongue, or forces
its phraseology in deference to the language translated, violates a golden rule and misapprehends the
true functions and purpose of poetry. Whatever
may be the merit of closely adhering to the letter
of the original, I apprehend that an approximation
to the spirit is of far greater consequence ; and I
find that an old English poet of the seventeenth

century has expressed himself on this subject so
admirably, that I cannot do better than quote his
words in support of my position.   In reference to
Fanshawe's version of Guarini, Sir John Denham
writes :—

> That servile path thou nobly dost decline,
> Of tracing word by word and line by line,
> Those are the laboured birth of slavish brains,
> Not the effect of poetry, but pains,
> Cheap vulgar arts, whose narrowness affords
> No flight for thoughts, but poorly stick at words :
> A new and nobler way thou dost pursue—
> To make translations and translators too ;
> They but preserve the ashes, thou the flame,
> True to his sense, but truer to his fame.

Need I say more?   If only my practice were equal
to his theory, or my own, further preface would be
superfluous ; but the practice of preachers is apt to
be below their own standard, and a translator's path
notoriously lies betwixt Scylla and Charybdis.   Few,
if any, have ever yet steered clear of the shoals on
either side, so it will be as well to apologize before-
hand for the aberrations of the pilot.   I trust that
my wish to be a faithful interpreter has not been
marred either by lack of care or any misapprehension
of my master's meaning : but *humanum est errare*.
If my rendering should, now and then, seem at

first sight to be somewhat loose, or the exigencies of rhyme should entail a few apparent interpolations, I trust that it will be found, on examination, that I have not unjustifiably paraphrased, or amplified, my master's own pregnant words. It will be for the critic to determine how far I have succeeded in what, to use the hackneyed expression, has been my labour of love. If I should obtain a verdict in my favour, I shall be well content ; if I should be so fortunate as to add any to the number of those who honor Dante's worshipful guide, I shall be well rewarded.

In adopting different variations of the ballad metres, and octosyllabics, I have been guided by my judgment of what appeared most suitable to the several lays. But I am inclined to regret not having made more use of the metre I have chosen for the seventh Eclogue, which appears to me peculiarly appropriate to this variety of poem. Professor Conington, in his admirable version of the Æneid, remarks that the number of syllables in two octosyllabic lines is very little in excess of the average number of syllables in an hexameter. The choice of a metre, containing the same number of syllables as the original, is, I think, very conducive to the faithfulness of a translation. Pregnant and concise

as the Latin has been always considered, our own
tongue will, if this test be applied, prove to be
a closer rival to it than it has usually been deemed.
It is too much to expect that our old heroic line
of ten syllables should comprise all that can be
said in an hexameter, which averages fifteen ; and
I take it to be a most mistaken idea to restrict
a translation to the identical number of lines of the
original, irrespective of their length.   This applies
with especial force to the Odes of Horace and
I regret to find my opinion here at variance with
that of Professor Conington.   The restriction may
sometimes lead to happy results, earning the credit
due to successful *tours de force*, but, as a rule, it is
apt to necessitate omissions, which are to be deprecated, far more, I think, than interpolations, which.
if judiciously, and *sparingly* introduced. and *indicated
by brackets*, appear to me to be a legitimate, if not
an indispensable, item among the resources of the
translator.   For every poet of necessity modifies
his phraseology according to the requirements of
his metre, and thinks out thoughts to replace such
as will not fit the space for which they were intended.
This is but the "*limæ labor*" preached and practised
by the great Professor Horace himself.   And can it
be supposed for a moment that, if the poet had

written in our own language, he would have retained precisely the same expressions, and the same metaphors, and excluded others which the genius of the language would have suggested to him? Assuredly not. And if we are to make his rhymes as acceptable to our contemporaries as he would have done—and that is surely the main object of a translation—a similar license must be conceded to us in this respect. It is the abuse, and not the use, of such a license which is, in my judgment, to be deprecated.

I have thought it not inappropriate to place within these boards a few of the Lyrics of the great master's no less distinguished friend. He has found so many interpreters of late, that it seemed superfluous to undertake another version of the whole. But I could see no valid reason why I should not attempt a few especial favourites from among them. While I have generally inclined to popular English measures, I have thought it not amiss to render some few odes into the original metres, abandoning rhyme for rhythm. The difficulties of the Alcaic are considerable, though not insurmountable ; but it is questionable how far the metre, even if mastered, will ever be naturalized. It certainly never can be popular, unless a natural system of prosody be adopted, which will enable it to be read, with ease and fluency, by those who are altogether unacquainted with the classical originals. I am not unconscious of the shortcomings of these experiments—but if I have not altogether fallen short of the standard of my predecessors, I shall have no reason to regret the few pleasant hours I have spent over my alluring task.

It only remains for me to record my obligations to several kind friends for their judicious criticisms, and especially to the Rev. G. W. Kitchin, of Ch. Ch., Oxon, for the trouble he has taken in looking through my proof-sheets, and for many valuable suggestions ; and, in conclusion, to express a hope that my reception on this new stage may not be such as to discourage my speedy reappearance on the boards.

T. HERBERT NOYES, JUNR.

UNITED UNIVERSITY CLUB,
    December, 1867.

THE BUCOLICS.

ARGUMENT.

When Octavian (afterwards Augustus Cæsar) had rewarded his veterans by a grant of confiscated land in the neighbourhood of Cremona and Mantua, Virgil, among others, was despoiled of his Mantuan estate, but recovered what he had lost through the interest of Asinius Pollio with Mecænas, and through him with Octavian. So, in this first Eclogue he sings the praises of Octavian, his own good fortune under the pseudonym of Tityrus, and the evil fortunes of the Mantuans represented by the exiled Melibœus.

Mel. Ah ! Tityrus, in this sweet glade
Beneath the beeches' branching shade,
'Tis thine to dream at ease, and woo
The sylvan muse, the summer through,
  Upon the rustic reed.
But we must quit our native land,
The fields we love, a homeless band,
Whilst thou dost make the groves around
Thine Amaryllid's name resound,
  Nor lack of leisure plead.   10
 Tit. Oh, Melibœus, he whose nod
Hath wrought this leisure is a God ;

B

At least, to me, will ever be,
Whatever betide, a Deity ;
For him our folds shall oft supply
A tender lamb foredoomed to die
Upon his altars, evermore
Imbrued with sacrificial gore.
For he it is who, as you see,
Hath left my kine at large, and me   20
At liberty to pipe and plead,
All day upon my rustic reed.

    Mel. Indeed, my friend, I grudge it not,
I rather marvel at thy lot,
Amid such ruin as prevails
Throughout these whilom happy dales.
I, but a feeble invalid,
My flock of milch-goats forth must speed,
Yet scarce can stir this one poor ewe,
For in this hazel copse she threw,   30
Just now, the promise of my flock—
Twin kidlings—on the barren rock,
Abandoned, as you see, to die !
What wonder, then, that I should sigh !
Now well I wot that, if my mind
Had not been once perversely blind,
Full oft the lightning-blasted oak,
And eke the boding raven's croak
From out the hollow ilex tree,
When I would neither hear nor see,   40
Predicted all these ills to me.

But, Tityrus, old friend, I pray
What Deity protects thee, say ?
   Tit. The city, friend, whose name is Rome,
I idly deemed like ours at home ;
Our Mantua, where, thou know'st it well,
The produce of our flocks we sell ;
So whelps I knew were like their dams,
So ewes were like the tender lambs,
And so I always thought it fair   50
Great things with little to compare ;
But soon I found that Rome, so vast,
All other cities far surpassed—
As cypresses, that soar so high,
The lowly osier brakes outvie.
   Mel. But tell me, now, what made thee go
To visit Rome ?   I fain would know.
   Tit. Freedom, which smiled at last, though
     late,
On me, submissive to my fate :
How late, why let the barber say   60
Who found my beard was tinged with grey.
'Twas when, by Amaryllid's smiles,
Released from Galatea's wiles,
I learnt the worth of liberty ;
For I must needs confess that I
     My hopes had all resigned,
And found my cash would never last
While Galatea held me fast
     Within her bonds confined.

Though many a victim from my fold   70
Was in the Mantuan market sold,
And busily my press would squeeze
For thankless cits a wealth of cheese,
It never was my lot to find
That wealth of gold remained behind.

   Mel. I know now, Amaryllis, why
So sadly thou wert wont to sigh,
Invoking Heaven, and allow
The fruit, dead ripe, to weight the bough :
It was that Tityrus could be   80
Impassive to thy sighs and thee !
The very springs, the very pines,
The very tendrils of the vines,
Oh ! faithless Tityrus, I see,
Were vainly beckoning to thee.

   Tit. What could I do ? I could not fly
My bondage, nor as yet descry
What good the Gods had yet in store
For me when all my woes were o'er.
But 'twas at Rome, my friend, I found   90
   The youth to me so justly dear ;
The youth for whom, as moons come round,
   My altars smoke twelve times a year :
'Twas he conceded me, so soon
As it was craved, the welcome boon :
" Go, feed your beeves, boys, as before,
And let your bulls be yoked once more."

   Mel. Well done, old friend ; I see the charm

By which thou dost retain thy farm !
A farm sufficient for thy need.   100
Though stony be the soil indeed,
Though crusty peat and treacherous bog
With slimy rush the pastures clog,
No bane of unaccustomed herbs
Those flocks of lambing ewes disturbs,
Nor murrain, brought by neighbouring kine,
Endangers those sleek beeves of thine ;
But here, my good old friend, it seems,
Beside the old familiar streams
And sacred springs, thou'lt still enjoy   110
Cool blissful shade without annoy ;
Here, by thy fringe of willows, where
The bees of Hybla oft repair
The luscious honey-dew to sip
Its blossoms offer to their lip,
Their constant hum will challenge sleep,
While o'er thy couch the willows weep ;
While from the crags upon the breeze
Vine-dressers fling wild melodies ;
And at the caves thy favourite doves   120
Exchange the stories of their loves ;
And turtles on the lofty elms
With cooings fill their leafy realms.

   Tit. Therefore the hinds shall first repair
To goodly pastures in the air,—
The teaming seas, alive no more,
Shall strand their fish upon the shore,—

The banished Parthian shall drink
His fill beside the Arar's brink,—
The German sip the Tigris' waves,   130
Transplanted to the realms it laves,
Before *his* image shall depart
The mindful mirror of my heart.

    Mel. But we to Afric's burning sands
Must wander off, and further lands :
To Scythia some, and some to Crete,
Where swift Oaxes' waters meet
The sea ; and some to Britain's coasts,
Which in its isolation boasts.
Oh ! shall I ever in lapse of time   140
Again behold my native clime ;
My humble cottage, with its roof
Of turf, securely weather-proof ?
My little farm, my own domain,
When shall I see your garbs again ?
Shall some wild trooper's wantonness
My own spruce tillage lands possess ?
Some rude barbarian reap my corn
While I am left bereft, forlorn ?
To what a pass hath civil strife   150
Reduced the burden of our life !
For whom have we poor wretches sown
The fields we fondly deemed our own ?
Go, Meliboeus, graft thy pears,
And range thy budding vines in layers.

My whilom happy flock, proceed,
My milch goats, follow, where I lead :
Henceforth no more where creepers twine
Round some green cave may I recline,
And all your agile tricks survey   160
While on the briery crags you play.
Henceforth no songs for me—no more
'It will be my lot to lead you o'er
The mountain paths, and bid you crop
The cytisus and willow top.

    Tit. Yet stay one night, my friend, with me ;
I'll strew a couch of leaves for thee :
Of mellow fruit I have a store,
Sweet chestnuts too, and, what is more,
Of curded milk a good supply ;   170
Already now the night is nigh ;
From distant chimneys, there, the smoke
Is curling up ; and, see, the oak
Throws lengthening shadows—from the hills
The spreading gloom the valley fills.

ECLOGUE II.—Alexis.

———*o*———

ARGUMENT.

The loves of two shepherds, Corydon and Alexis. Corydon commences with a complaint that Alexis spurns him, and proceeds to boast of his wealth, his musical talents, and his personal appearance. He celebrates the praises of a rural life, promises him liberal presents, and finally reproaches himself with his folly, and returns to his home pursuits.

The shepherd Corydon's chief joy
Was fair Alexis—lovely boy—
His lord's delight ; tho' all in vain
He strove the youthful heart to gain,
But none the less would he frequent
The beech-groves, dense of shade, intent
On trilling this, his artless song,
The lonely hills and glades among.
" Cruel Alexis ! Why despise
The burden of my songs and sighs ?   10
Hast thou no pity to bestow ?
Wouldst drive me to the shades below ?
Now even the flocks for shade retreat
To cool dark groves and shun the heat ;

And all the emerald lizards fly
For refuge to the brambles nigh ;
While Thestylis is pounding, see,
The garlic-cloves, and betony
With garden herbs, good viands meet
For reapers wearied with the heat.　　　20
But as for me, while I pursue
　　Beneath the scorching sun's fierce beam
Thy flying steps the noontide through
　　I hear but shrill tree-crickets scream !
Oh ! was it not enough, and more,
To suffer as I did before,
When Amaryllid's cold disdain
And peevish passion was my bane ?
Menalcas too, that faithless friend !
(When will my many troubles end ?)　　　30
Yet boast not, boy, thy golden hair,
Tho' he was dark, and thou art fair ;
Unmarked fair privet berries fall,—
Black bilberries are dear to all.
I count for nothing in thine eyes !
Alexis ! witless of thy prize,
Thou heedest not my depth of sighs.
What wealth of flocks, what dairy store,
What streams of milk are mine ! What's more,
A thousand little lambs for me　　　40
Upon Sicilian hills there be ;
New milk in summer fills my cans,
Nor yet in winter fail my pans ;

The songs Amphion used to sing,
Who made the echoing welkin ring ;
What time he called his kine to leave
The Aracynthian slopes at eve ;—
I sing them all.   And then, confess,
I am not void of comeliness,
For lately, standing on the shore,   50
I scanned the glassy mirror o'er,
And saw my image in the sea ;
And, if its witness faithful be,
I fear not Daphnid's rivalry !
Oh ! would it were thy will to share
My humble roof, my humbler fare ;
With me pursue the fleet wild roe,
Or drive the kids where mallows grow :
Along with me in wood and lea
To mimic Pan in minstrelsy.   60
For Pan it was erst showed the way
To join with wax the reeds we play ;
And Pan it is who guards our folds,
And us, their masters, harmless holds.
Then, prithee, why my Art disdain ?
And from the pipes thy lips refrain ?
Who knows not what unflagging zeal
Amyntas for his task could feel ?
A pipe compactly framed I own,
Seven reeds well tuned, of perfect tone :   70
Long since Damœtas gave it me,
And dying said, ' 'Tis thou wilt be

The second master it has had,'
And envy made Amyntas sad.
Moreover, two young roes I feed,
Two little roes of mountain breed,
Which in a dangerous glen I caught,
And hardly to my homestead brought—
Their sides already flecked with white—
They drain one ewe's two udders quite : 80
Long since have they been begged of
    me
By Thestylis, but kept for thee !
But soon I'll yield them to her sighs
Since thou dost all my gifts despise.
Come hither, then, my lovely boy,
Behold the nymphs, no longer coy,
For thee their brimming vases bear
All crowned with lilies sweetly fair ;
The lovely Naïad plucks for thee
White violets and rosemary, 90
And in her hearty zeal to please
Adds vermeil poppy-heads to these,
With hyacinths and yellow dill,
Whose blossoms balmy scents distil ;
And deftly blends with sober flowers
Rich marigolds in golden showers.
Their gift with quinces I will crown,
Hoar quinces clad with velvet down ;
And chestnuts too, so dear you know
To Amaryllis long ago ; 100

I'll add some golden plums to these ;
These apples too may chance to please ;
These fronds of bay I'll pluck in turn,
This myrtle next, in hopes to earn
The favour that my heart entreats
By studied interchange of sweets.
Poor Corydon 's a country lout ;
Alexis can well do without
Such gifts as his and if, indeed,
It is with gifts he hopes to plead,   110
How hard soever he may try
With Julius can he hope to vie ?
Fool that I am !—what have I done ?
Methinks that all my wits are gone !
I have let the wind among the flowers,
The pigs in these pure founts of ours !
Whom, madman, are you fleeing now ?
The Gods once dwelt in woods, I trow ;
And Paris too.   Let Pallas dwell   120
In her own chosen citadel ;
The woods for me ! that life so free,
The sylvan life is the life for me !
The savage lioness pursues
The wolf: the wolf itself will choose
The goat for food, that wanton chews
The cytisus, sweet harmless flower ;
And Corydon this very hour
Pursues Alexis to his bower !
Each one pursues his own delight,   130

Whatever is pleasing in his sight.
See now the beeves returning here
Their plough-shares all thrown out of gear,
And now the setting sun invades
The landscape with its lengthening shades ;
Yet love still rages in my breast ;
Can any bounds love's course arrest ?
Ah, Corydon ! poor Corydon !
What phrenzy moves thee, simpleton ?
Upon the untrimmed elm thy vine   140
Is left, I see, half-dressed to twine !
Come then, no longer now disdain
To weave with lithesome rush or cane
Some handy household implement,
Nor let thy time be all misspent.
What if Alexis deal thee scorn,
Thou wilt not long be left forlorn."

ECLOGUE III.—Palæmon.

———o———

ARGUMENT.

  This Eclogue, which is an imitation of the fourth and fifth Idylls of Theocritus, purports to be the record of a musical competition between two shepherds, Menalcas and Damœtas, Palæmon intervening as umpire. It has been held that Virgil intended Damœtas to personate himself, and Menalcas some now unknown rival. Asinius Pollio, whose praises it celebrates incidentally, was governor of the Mantuan territory about A.C. 43, which is supposed to be the date of the composition of the Eclogue.

Men. Whose flocks are these, Damœtas, say,
Doth Melibœus own them, pray?
  Dam. Not so, but Ægon; it was he
Who gave them all in charge to me.
  Men. Oh ever luckless flock! poor sheep!
While he is doubtless gone to keep
A watch on Neæra, in his fright
Lest I should prove her dear delight!
This stranger's hand will surely milk
The hapless ewes twice o'er, and bilk   10

The flock of half its dues, and cheat
The lambkins of their wonted teat.

   Dam. Such slanderous taunts 'twere best to
     throw
More sparingly, I'd have you know.
Of you we know a thing or two,
What late our goat-herds saw you do !
What honour in the nymph's fair shrine
You pleased to pay to things divine !

   Men. No doubt 'twas when I chanced to see
Poor Mico's vineyard cruelly   20
Maltreated, and each tender vine
All hacked about with fell design.

   Dam. Or when by that old beech, you know,
You broke poor little Daphnid's bow
And arrow, no long while ago,
For envy, which you felt so soon
As he received the welcome boon !
If you had had no tooth to bite
You would soon, I'm sure, have died of spite !

   Men. Whatever will our masters do   30
When thieves have got so daring too !
Did I not see you, rascal, aim
At catching Damon's goat ? For shame !
Lycisca barked the while hard by,
And when I cried Hi ! Tityrus, hi !
Wherever did the rascal fly ?
Drive in the flock—behind the hedge
You lurked the while among the sedge.

Dam. And why should not the vanquished
  pay
The prize my pipe had won me, pray ? 40
That goat was mine of right, you know,
Damon himself avowed it so,
While he denied his power to pay.

 Men. Your pipe! it vanquished him, you say?
As if, forsooth, you had e'er been worth
A pipe since first you cumbered earth !
Yet stay, I had forgotten, true,
The bungler at the crossways, who
Of late upon a squeaking straw
Was wont to ply his tuneless jaw ! 50

 Dam. Well, then, suppose that you and I
Each others' skill at once should try ;
I'll stake this heifer—without fail
Twice daily faithful to the pail,—
Twin calves she suckles ; who would choose
So notable a prize refuse ?
But tell us now what stake you wage ?

 Men. I would not venture on a gage
From this my flock—for I've, in truth,
A sire at home, and, to my ruth, 60
A stepmother—and twice a day
They count the flock ; whate'er I say,
One counts the kids—they never fail—
The other takes the hoggets' tale.
But yet I fain would gratify
Your madness, though it aim so high ;

Two beechen flagons I will stake,
Alcimedon's, his famous make,
Well fashioned on the facile lathe;
The vine-leaves, mixed with ivy, swathe   70
Their rim with wreaths and berries there,
And clustering grapes attest his care.
Below two central figures stand,
Chased richly by his master hand,
Great Conon* there, and he who well
Described the globe whereon we dwell,
And all its seasons, when the plough,—
And when the sickle rules, and how:
As yet untouched by lips are they,
Both kept securely stowed away.   80

Dam. The same Alcimedon for me
Two flagons made, as you shall see;
Acanthus wreath their handles knits,
Their central figure, Orpheus, sits;
The green woods follow in his train;
A worthier prize you would seek in vain.
Quite innocent of lips are they,
Both kept quite snugly stowed away;
But if my heifer 'tis you want,
Your flagons all in vain you vaunt.   90

Men. Think not to 'scape me so at all,
On any terms I'm yours at call;
Here comes Palæmon, we are three,
The judge between us he shall be;

* A friend of Archimedes.

I'll take good care your voice shall bane
No gentle ears henceforth again.

   Dam. Come, then, if you have aught to say,
It is not I who would delay,
Afraid of none am I ; but, friend
Palæmon, you must comprehend   100
Of how much moment is the fray :
So give it all your heed, I pray.

   Pal. Proceed, now we have found a seat
Upon the turf so soft and sweet ;
The season this for every field
And every tree its best to yield ;
The woods are green ; we see the year
In grandest gala suit appear.
Do you, Damœtas, lead the way ;
Menalcas follow with your lay ;   110
Alternately your lays recite,
Alternate strains the Muse delight.

Dam.

Jove is the true primeval source,
   He makes the cornlands bear ;
All things from Jove derive their force,
   He makes my lays his care.

Men.

But I to Phœbus most am dear,
   His gifts are my heirloom,

His bays upon my brow I wear,
  His hyacinthine bloom.   120

Dam.

'Tis Galatea, wanton minx,
  Pelts me with fruit and flies
Towards the willows, where she thinks
  And longs to catch my eyes.

Men.

Amyntas is the friend so dear
  Who never flies from me ;
Not Delia's self, so oft she is here,
  My dogs more often see.

Dam.

Gifts ready for my love have I,
  For I have marked the spot   130
Where wheeling flights of ring-doves fly,
  Beside a sylvan grot.

Men.

Ten golden quinces plucked for me
  I have sent my love to-day,
The best I could—to-morrow she
  Shall have the rest, I say.

Dam.

My love's own wealth of whispers I
  So sweet and pleasant find,
I often think they ought to fly
  To Heaven upon the wind.   140

C 2

Men.

What boots it that you spurn me not,
  If with the hounds you ride,
Amyntas, while I am oft forgot,
  And with the nets must bide.

Dam.

My birthday 'tis—my Phillis send
  To glad me with her eyes,
You, too, Iulus must attend
  My harvest sacrifice.

Men.

I love sweet Phillis most of all,
  It is the truth I tell,   150
She wept my footsteps to recall,
  And sighed one long farewell.

Dam.

The wolf 's a caution to the fold,
  The tempest to the tree,
To ripened fruit the showers cold,
  Amaryllid's wrath to me.

Men.

Soft rain to growing corn is sweet,
  Limp withes to lambing ewes,
Kids deem the arbutus a treat,
  Amyntas I would choose.   160

Dam.

'Tis Pollio loves my rustic Muse,
  Though homely it appear ;
Kind Muses, do not then refuse
  For him a calf to rear.

Men.

But Pollio's self can sonnets write,
  So he must have a steer,
Who with his horns and hoofs can fight,
  And fling sand far and near.

Dam.

Who loves thee, Pollio, let him go
  Where thou hast won the palm ;   170
For him let streams of honey flow,
  The brambles bear him balm.

Men.

Who hates not Bavius let him love
  With Mævius to sigh ;
Let him yoke foxes too, sweet dove !
  And milk the he-goat dry.

Dam.

Ho ! boys, that cull the flowers—take care !
  Fly quickly, boys,—I quake !
Come, leave your flowers and strawberries there,
  The grass conceals a snake !   180

Men.

Haste not, my ewes, so fast, but stay,
　　For see the ram your guide,
(The treacherous banks have given way),
　　He shakes his dripping hide.

Dam.

Go, Tityrus, drive the goats away,
　　They are browsing on the bank ;
I'll take them all myself some day,
　　And wash them in the tank.

Men.

Drive home the ewes, lad : should the heat
　　Once strike my poor milch ewes,　　　　190
As erst, in vain we'll strain the teat,
　　Their milk we'll surely lose.

Dam.

Was ever bull so lean as mine
　　Among such rich lucerne ?
'Tis love that makes the cattle pine,
　　And makes the master burn.

Men.

It is not love my lambkins harms,
　　They are but bones and skin ;
I wish I knew whose evil charms
　　Have made them all so thin.　　　　200

Dam.

Come, tell me, and I'll vote you now
Apollo's wreath to grace your brow,
Where in the world can you descry
No more than just three ells of sky ?

Men.

Where in the world, come, tell me now,
And Phillis shall be yours I vow,
Are monarchs' names who reign on earth
Inscribed on fairy flowers at birth ?

Pal. It cannot be, my friends, that I
Betwixt your merits should descry,   210
Whether of prosperous loves your song,
Or darker days when all went wrong
(But if the verdict I pronounce,
I say the scale swerves not an ounce) ;
And both deserve alike, I find,
A heifer with bay-wreaths entwined.
Shut up the sluices, lads, indeed
The meadows now have all they need !

ECLOGUE IV.—Pollio.

———*0*———

ARGUMENT.

This remarkable Eclogue was expounded by no less a person than Constantine the Great, as a prophecy of the Messiah's coming! It was afterwards thought by some to be an adulatory prophecy of the fortunes of an expected child of the poet's patron, Pollio. Mr. Granville Penn published a volume to prove that it was really a poem in honour of Augustus Cæsar, written A.C. 39, when the peace of Brundusium had laid the foundations of his Imperial power. Mr. Penn holds that the whole poem, after the first four lines, is to be interpreted as proceeding from the mouth of the Cumæan Sibyll.

1.

Come, Muse of Etna, let us chant
  A somewhat loftier lay,
We do not all for ever pant
  In tamarisk scrub to play.

2.

If forests needs must be our theme,
  Imperial glades we'll choose ;
The age that crowned the Sibyll's dream
  Is come—proclaim the news.

3.

The world's vast cycle once again
　Begins its course anew,
The Virgin now returns to reign,
　Now Saturn's reign is due.

10

4.

A babe of heaven is born on earth,
　Blest guerdon of the sky !
Lucina, do thou bless his birth,
　Thy Phœbus reigns on high !

5.

He is the babe in whom, I ween,
　The iron age expires ;
The age of gold will soon be seen
　To crown our hearts' desires.

20

6.

Great Pollio, 'tis thy consulate
　Will see this age begin,
The illustrious file is at the gate,
　The file of months steps in.

7.

All traces of what sins remain
　To mar our happy earth,
Effaced in thy propitious reign,—
　No fears will frighten mirth.

8.

Thou babe, the heir of life divine,
  The demigods wilt see,   30
Commingled with the heavenly line,
  And seen of them wilt be.

9.

Thou'lt rule, with all thy father's worth,
  The world in peace at last,
While at thy feet the sons of earth
  Their first-fruits freely cast.

10.

The earth untilled will not withhold
  From thee its gifts of balm,
And cassia, worth its weight in gold,
  Acanthus wreaths and palm.   40

11.

With brimming dugs the ewes will fare
  Unbidden to the fold ;
The lion's roar will fail to scare
  The herds, securely bold.

12.

Thy very cradle, too, will bud,
  And burst forth into bloom ;
The earth will drink the serpent's blood,
  And poisonous herbs consume.

13.

Then everywhere, in every mead,
　The Assyrian balm will spring,　　　50
(And every noxious germ and seed
　From this our globe take wing).

14.

So soon thou canst the annals read
　Of thine ancestral line,
And prove that virtue is indeed
　In quality divine.

15.

The ripening ears of corn will turn
　To gold upon the earth,
(And all discordant chords will learn
　The harmonies of mirth).　　　60

16.

Then by the rugged paths the grape,
　The sweet blush grape, will sway,
And eke the hardy oaks agape
　Their honeyed stores display.

17.

Yet haply of the ancient vice
　Some traces will survive,
Which mortal men will still entice
　With ocean's might to strive.

18.

Walls still shall girdle cities then,
  The spade still score the lea,   70
The ploughshare still will busy men,
  Sailors still tempt the sea.

19.

With other pilots at the helm,
  New Argos then will speed,
To waft the heroes of the realm
  In other wars to bleed.

20.

For other wars there yet must be
  (The antidote of joy);
The great Achilles we shall see
  Again despatched to Troy.   80

21.

But later, when of age mature,
  Thou donn'st the virile gown,
(When on thy brow there rests secure
  The glory of a crown),

22.

The merchant then will wholly cease
  To cross the briny sea ;
No merchandise in time of peace
  For barter there will be.

23.

For every soil will freely bear
　All produce on its breast;　　　90
No harrow then the field will tear;
　The pruning-hook will rest.

24.

The sturdy ploughman, too, will free
　His oxen from the yoke;
(No more for toil of husbandry
　Their steaming sides will smoke).

25.

No wool will then be taught to feign
　The tints of varied dyes;
His fleece the ram himself will stain
　To pleasure his own eyes.　　　100

26.

With hyacinthine purple now,
　And now with crocus gold—
Nature herself will paint, I trow,
　The lambkins of the fold.

27.

For thus, in harmony with fate,
　The Parcæ have decreed,
" In its own cycle at due date
　Let such an age succeed."

28.

Then haste thy coming, babe divine,
    Great son of highest Jove;   110
Assume the honours that are thine,
    Dear infant of our love.

29.

Behold the world inclining low
    Beneath its heavenly load;
Earth, sea, and heaven saluting bow
    (In unaccustomed mode).

30.

See all creation joyous hail
    The glorious coming age;
Oh, may my span of years not fail,
    Nor turn life's latest page;   120

31.

Nor breath run short, ere I have time
    To celebrate thy name,
In fitting staves of faultless rhyme
    To herald forth thy fame.

32.

Then neither Orpheus, he of Thrace,
    In song shall rival me,
Nor Linus, though their parents' grace
    Should aid their progeny.

33.

And 'twas the muse, Calliope,
  Gave noble Orpheus birth :   130
Apollo's faultless symmetry
  Gave Linus to the earth.

34.

Should Pan himself the contest dare
  Our umpire Arcady,
To Pan would Arcady declare
  That he must yield to me.

35.

Come, babe, return her smiles, and cheer
  Thy own fond mother's heart ;
These ten long months for thee, I fear,
  Have borne her many a smart.   140

36.

Come, babe ! The wight whose parents spare
  Such* smiles their love to vouch,
His future feasts no God will share,
  No goddess grace his couch.

---

* Attia, the mother of Augustus, claimed Venus for her an-
cestress. The myth lent a special value to her smiles divine.
—(*Vide* Penn., p. 94.)

ECLOGUE V.—DAPHNIS.

——o——

ARGUMENT.

Two shepherds, Mopsus and Menalcas, competing in rival songs, celebrate the praises of Daphnis, their lost friend. There nas been some difference of opinion as to the identity of the personage represented by Daphnis. Some have identified him with the Sicilian shepherd, in whose honour Theocritus wrote his first Idyll; others with the son of Pollio, to whom they believe the preceding Eclogue was intended to refer; others have even referred it to the Saviour. But Scaliger is doubtless right, who considers that Daphnis is no other than Julius Cæsar, to whom divine honours were decreed by the Triumvirs in A. U. C. 712, at a time when Brutus and Cassius were still in the field; and it was not impolitic to veil his name under that of a Sicilian shepherd.

1.

WHY, Mopsus, now that we have met,
    Both masters of our arts,
One on the pipes no mean adept,
    One good at song in parts.

2.

3 Why not beneath these elms, among
    The hazels here recline,
And in some little flights of song
    Our energies combine ?

3.

'Tis thine, Menalcas, to command,
 Mine rather to obey;   10
But why, by draughty breezes fanned,
 In shade so chequered stay?

4.

Why not to that sweet grot repair,
 See, round its mouth there twine
The tendrils fair, the clusters rare
 Of that unkempt wild vine.

5.

Men. Tut, Mopsus, thro' our hills alone
 With thee Amyntas vies.
Mop. And he with Phœbus, I must own,
 Might well dispute the prize. 20

6.

Men. Begin then, Mopsus, first recite
 Our Phillid's flames to-day;
Or Alcon's prowess, or the fight
 Which Codrus fought, I pray.

7.

Begin, the browsing kids for us
 Our Tityrus will mind.
Mop. Well, hear this song—I wrote it thus
 Upon the green beech rind.

D

8.

And harmonized it as I lay,
    Noting in turn the tune;   30
Come, listen, and maybe you 'will say
    We 'will beat Amyntas soon.

9.

Men. So far the humble osiers yield
    To olives pale the palm;
Or pinky willow herbs afield,
    To rosebeds breathing balm.

10.

So far we readily declare
    Amyntas yields to thee—
Mop. Enough, such homage, lad, forbear—
    Here in the cave are we.   40

11.

The cruel death of Daphnis dear
    The Nymphs were wont to wail;
Ye hazel groves, ye streamlets here
    Saw ceaseless grief prevail.

12.

What time his weeping mother fell
    Upon his woeful face;
Blaming the stars, and Heaven as well,
    Between each wild embrace.

13.

No herdsmen in those days for grief
    Drove cattle to the pool,   50
That so their thirst might find relief
    In waters fresh and cool.

14.

The very beasts themselves forbore
    Their appetites to sate ;
Even the Punic lions sore
    Bewailed thy hapless fate.

15.

The mountains, Daphnis, clad with oak,
    Dank forests moaned for thee,
Armenian tigers from thy yoke
    Cared little to be free.   60

16.

'Twas Daphnis led the circling dance
    Of Bacchanalian bands ;
And wreathed the thyrsus and the lance
    With foliage-twisted strands.

17.

As vines upon the sheltering trees :—
    As grapes upon the vine :—
As corn among the smiling leas :—
    As bulls among the kine :—

18.

Even so thou ever wert of thine
   The matchless grace and crown ;   70
And when at last the Fates malign
   Swept all thy glory down,

19.

Then Pales left the fields—her care,
   Apollo left them too ;
Now all that is noxious harbours there
   Where golden treasures grew.

20.

The furrows where good barley seed
   Once carefully was sown,
With vile wild oats and darnel weed
   Are now all overgrown.   80

21.

Where once was scented violet bloom,
   And purple daffodil,
Sharp thorns and thistles in their room
   The rugged landscape fill.

22.

Come shepherd, strew the ground with flowers,
   And where cool fountains flow,
Go plant for shelter shady bowers,
   Good Daphnis willed it so.

23.

And rear for him a tomb, and write
  This epitaph thereon—   90
[That all who pass the sacred site
  The happy rhymes may con.]

24.

" Daphnis am I—the starry host
  My bruited fame could see ;
No fairer flock than mine could boast
  A fairer hind than me."

25.

Men. As on the meads the overflow
  Of brooks in summer time ;
As sleep, the antidote of woe,
  Upon a bed of thyme.   100

26.

So falls thy song, oh bard divine,
  Most sweetly on our ears ;
This heavenly melody of thine
  Our inmost spirit cheers.

27.

As well in music as in song,
  Thy master's rival now,
My fortune-favoured youth, ere long
  Thou'lt be his peer, I vow.

28.

But now it 'is time that we in turn
  Begin to tune our lay,   110
In praise of thy good Daphnis, learn
  That we have much to say.

29.

His fame we fain would celebrate,
  And hymn it to the sky,
For Daphnis loved us also, mate,—
  That is the reason why !

30.

Mop. What higher prize could be bestowed
  That we could well receive ?
And who so worthy of an ode
  As he for whom we grieve.   120

31.

'Twas Stimicon, some while ago,
  Who came and brought us word
How sweetly all thy stanzas flow,
  Which he had lately heard.

32.

Men. Our Daphnis, now a child of light,
  To Heaven's gate draws near,
The clouds, the stars—a wondrous sight-
  Beneath his feet appear.

33.

And this is why the fields rejoice,
    The country shouts for joy,   130
And teeming woodlands all their voice
    In melody employ.

34.

And this is why in pastoral choir
    Great Pan himself is glad,
And Nymphs and Dryads all aspire
    Their symphony to add.

35.

And this is why the wolves forbear
    To chase the timid sheep ;
And no vile toils the wild deer scare :
    He would that none should weep.   140

36.

The very rugged hills for joy
    Their choral voices raise ;
The very rocks themselves employ
    Their echoes in his praise.

37.

The very coppices proclaim
    That he is now divine ;
Then come, Menalcas, bless his name,
    And rear for him a shrine.

38.

Do thou propitious be, and kind,
    Thine aid, good Daphnis, deign :   150
Four shrines are here—and two designed
    For thee—for Phœbus twain.

39.

Two bowls of milk fresh filled for thee,
    An annual offering ;
Two vases full as they can be
    Of purest oil I'll bring.

40.

At many a joyous banquet, too,
    The rosy wine shall flow,
In shady groves the summer thro',
    Beside the hearth, in snow.   160

41.

For thee new nectar shall distil
    From the Arvisian vine ;
Good Ægon and Damœtas trill
    For thee their notes divine.

42.

Alphesibœus, too, shall ape
    The Satyr's dance for thee ;
For thee all honours of the grape
    And all festivity.

43.

So oft the Dryads' feast comes round,
 So oft the lustral rites,   170
So long as fish in streams abound,
 And game on mountain heights.

44.

So long as bees delight in thyme,
 And grasshoppers in dew,
Thy name, thy praise in every clime,
 Our memories shall imbue.

45.

As now to Bacchus rustics pay,
 And Ceres annual vows,
So now henceforth thy name, I say,
 Their fealty shall arouse.   180

46.

Mop. What gifts shall now my thanks express
 For such a song as thine,
For not the wild wind's wantonness,
 With all its charm divine ;

47.

Nor yet the throbbing of the waves
 Upon the answering shore ;
Nor yet the gurgling brook that laves
 The pebbles evermore ;

48.

Could ever yet to me afford
  Such raptures of delight,⁣   190
As these melodious strains out-poured
  From thy kind lips to-night !

49.

Men. Yet first from us this fragile reed
  Our gift, accept, we pray ;
It oft hath earned us goodly meed
  In many a former lay.

50.

On this we sang " Young Corydon,
  The lonely Shepherd's joy,"
We sang of Ægon's sheep upon
  This very reed, my boy.   200

51.

Mop. Do thou accept from me this crook,
  To many a suit denied,
For it, with many a wistful look,
  Antigenes hath sighed,

52.

In vain, although a valued friend,
  Menalcas, it is thine ;
'Tis knotted well from end to end,
  And shod with brass so fine.

ECLOGUE VI.—Silenus.

———o———

ARGUMENT.

This Eclogue is dedicated to the same Varus to whom Horace addressed the eighteenth ode of his first Book. It was, no doubt, to pleasure him as an Epicurean that he puts into the mouth of Silenus, the demigod, a discourse on the tenets of that philosophy, and sundry mythological legends which would have been somewhat out of place in the mouth of a shepherd.

I.

Our muse did not at first disdain
  Sicilian airs to play,
Nor blushed among her rustic train
  In sylvan scenes to stray.

2.

Nay, when we first inclined to make
  Wars' episodes our care,
Apollo touched our ear, and spake,
  " Good Tityrus, beware."

3.

" A careful shepherd it beseems
  His own sleek flock to tend,
On plain and unpretending themes
  His lyric powers to spend."

4.

So now upon my slender reed
    I 'will practise rustic lays,
For, Varus, there are bards indeed
    Enough to sing thy praise.

5.

Enough to sing of warriors—I
    My monitor obey,
Yet should some sympathetic eye
    Peruse my simple lay,   20

6.

Our tamarisks, Varus, I'll engage,
    Our groves shall sing of thee ;
Aye, to the God of Lyres no page
    Will more delightful be,

7.

Than that to which thy noble name,
    Prefixed, its light shall lend.
Proceed, ye Muses, with the game
    Of Chromis and his friend.

8.

Mnasilus, who once haply caught
    Silenus sound asleep,   30
Within the grotto he had sought
    Fresh from potations deep,

9.

As was his wont.   The wreath he wore
  Had fallen off his head,
And lay neglected on the floor ;
  His full jug by his bed,

10.

With well-worn handles.   Him they seized,
  And bound— his wreath their thong :
For had he not, though often teased,
  Delayed their promised song ?   40

11.

The fair nymph Ægle's timid grace
  Came shyly to their side,
And helped to stain his brow and face
  With mulberry-juice applied.

12.

He, waking, asks, with laughter, " Why,
  Why bind me thus at all ?
Release me, lads ; enough that I
  Have seemed to be your thrall.

13.

The melodies you fain would hear,
  I'll sing them now for you.   50
Some other boon for Ægle here
  I'll shortly find her too."

14.

No sooner said than he began—
    'Twas marvellous to see—
Innumerable Satyrs ran,
    And frisked about in glee.

15.

The very oaks began to nod
    Their rigid tops in time ;
Parnassus hailed not so the God
    Of Lyres in his prime.   60

16.

So Ismarus did never yet
    For Orpheus, loved so well ;
So Rhodope would oft forget
    To recognize his spell.

17.

For as he sang he told us how
    The germs of earth, and sea,
And fire, and all that breathes below,
    Through space were wont to flee.

18.

And how, from such their elements,
    All things at prime were made,   70
Until the globe's magnificence
    Stood forth at last displayed.

19.

Then first the soil grew hard and dry,
    And set the bounds of seas,
And all that lives beneath the sky
    Was fashioned by degrees.

20.

'It was then that earth, amazed, beheld
    The sunlight's earliest dawn ;
Then first the welcome showers welled
    From cloudlets upward drawn.   80

21.

Then first the woods began to sprout,
    And yield a welcome shade ;
Beasts rare as yet to prowl about
    Each new-found hill and glade.

22.

He told what stones once Pyrrha threw ;
    In Saturn's glorious reign ;
Told of the ravening vultures, too,
    Prometheus' theft and pain.

23.

Of Hylas, too—the drowned—whose name
    Re-echoed from the shore,   90
What time his searching shipmates came,
    Who found him—never more.

24.

And all about Pasiphäe,
　Who loved the snow-white steer,
Who, had she never chanced to see
　A herd, had known more cheer.

25.

Alas ! what novel madness so
　Possessed thee, hapless maid !
But next he sang their kindred woe,
　Whose lowings filled the glade.　　　　100

26.

Poor Prœto's daughters, who believed
　Themselves transformed to kine,
And though less cruelly deceived,
　Yet feared they must resign

27.

Their shoulders to the ploughman's yoke,
　And sought in daily doubt
Upon their foreheads—'tis no joke—
　To feel the long horns sprout.

28.

Oh, hapless maid ! upon the hills
　Thou sighest still, maybe ;　　　　110
Thy steer the while his gullet fills
　Without a thought of thee !

29.

Or on some hyacinthine bed,
  Luxuriously reclined,
Lies ruminating, where o'erhead
  Dark ilex boughs are twined.

30.

Or from the jealous herd, maybe,
  Some favourite pursues :
" Kind Cretan nymphs, enlighten me,
  And give me of his news ;   120

31.

Close in the glades, that we may seek
  His footprints in the reeds ;
It well may be, in some mad freak,
  He's off to other meads ;

32.

That some fair heifers have decoyed
  Their far too willing thrall,
And led him off quite overjoyed
  To some Gortynian stall."

33.

And then he sang the' Hesperian fruit,
  And her it led astray ;   130
Thy daughters, too, he dared to bruit,
  Rash Phaeton, they say,

E

34.

The maidens who were sudden found
   Encased in mossy bark,
And firmly rooted in the ground,
   Tall alder trees of mark.

35.

To Gallus next the minstrel strayed,
   Whom, by Permesso's rills,
A muse encountered, and conveyed
   To her Aonian hills.   140

36.

And told how all the virgin nine
   To do him honour rose,
How Linus, stirred with fire divine,
   Their purpose did disclose.

37.

Thus Linus, crowned with wreath of flowers,
   And aromatic thyme :
" The muses [in their native bowers,
   Which thou hast learnt to climb]

38.

Present thee with these reeds of theirs ;
   Accept them—they are thine ;   150
'Twas Hesiod owned them once—his airs
   We know were all divine.

39.

The sturdy mountain ash with these
   From mountain heights he'd bring ;
Gryneum's grove with these thou'wilt please,
   The sacred grove to sing.

40.

So sing that in no other grove,
   In all the world beside,
Apollo shall so care to rove,
   Or feel such honest pride."   160

41.

Why tell how well he told the tale
   Of Scylla, widely known,
Who, 'midst the howling monsters pale,
   Which served her for a zone,

42.

Ulysses' fated vessels drew
   Within the whirlpool's bounds,
And tore to rags the frightened crew
   Among her fierce sea hounds.

43.

Or Tereus' legend ; and how changed
   In form his every limb,   170
What dainties Philomela ranged
   On tables set for him.

44.

How to the wilderness she fled
   So soon the truth he knew ;
How over his own roof he sped,
   And with what wings he flew.

45.

'Twas just as Phœbus chanted erst
   The very selfsame lays ;
Eurotas heard them sung, and durst
   Confide them to his bays.   180

46.

Thence learnt, he sang [till every bird
   Was hushed in mute surprise] ;
He sang, the echoing valleys heard,
   And told the listening skies.

47.

He sang till Hesperus bade them take
   Their cattle home to bed,
And made the lord of light forsake
   His azure throne o'erhead.

ECLOGUE VII.—Melibœus.

——o——

ARGUMENT.

This Eclogue, which appears to be founded on the eighth Idyll of Theocritus, records a vocal competition between two shepherds, Corydon and Thyrsis, in the presence of Daphnis and Melibœus. The latter officiates as umpire, and assigns the palm to Corydon.

1.

Mel. Beneath a whispering ilex
  It chanced that Daphnis lay,
Where Corydon and Thyrsis,
  Had led their flocks that day.
One owned the sheep, the other
  Goats destined for the pail ;
Both in the prime of manhood,
  Both of the Arcadian vale.

2.

Both skilled in song, and either
  For either part prepared ;   10
'It was thither that the patriarch
  Of all my goats had fared ;

While I was busy shielding
  My myrtles from the frost,
'Twas so I spied good Daphnis,
  Who knew what I had lost.

3.

And cried, " Here, Meliboeus,
  Your goats, your kids have strayed ;
They are safe—then if at leisure
  Come share our pleasant shade.   20
Your steers across the meadow
  Will come themselves to drink,
Here where the Mincio's rushes
  Conceal his verdant brink.

4.

Here, where the bees are swarming
  About the old oak tree."
What could I do ? No Phillis,
  No Alcippe for me
Was left to nurse my weanlings,
  Or shut my lambkins in ;   30
And Corydon and Thyrsis
  Were eager to begin.

5.

So I for once abandoned
  My business for their play ;
They with alternate stanzas
  At once began the fray.

The Muses love part singing,
  Wherein they both were versed,
So Thyrsis took the second,
  And Corydon the first.   40

6.

Cor. Ye Heliconian darlings,
  Your faithful bard inspire,
As Codrus erst who rivalled
  The patron of the lyre.
If with the highly favoured
  Such boon may not be mine,
My pipes for ever silent
  Shall grace this hallowed pine.

7.

Thy. For your young bard, ye shepherds,
  Come, weave an ivy crown,   50
That Codrus, late his rival,
  May wear an envious frown ;
Or else with some charmed chaplet
  Protect us from his praise,
Lest his malignant utterance
  Bewitch our future lays.

8.

Cor. Young Mico brings thee, Dian,
  This bristling wild-boar's head,
This pair of branching antlers
  That some fine stag has shed ;   60

A polished marble statue
    Shall be my gift, I swear,
With purple buskins garnished,
    If thou wilt hear my prayer.

                9.

Thy. This bowl of milk, Priapus,
    This dish of cakes each year,
For such a sorry garden
    Is all thy tithe, I fear:
Thy image now is marble,
    'It was all we could afford,   70
But should our flocks prove fruitful,
    In gold thou'wilt be adored.

                10.

Cor. Oh, Galatea Nerina,
    Than Hybla's sweets more rare,
More lovely than white ivy,
    Than fairest swan more fair :
So soon the steers from pasture
    Come trotting home to rest,
If Corydon'is your darling,
    Come, nestle on his breast.   80

                11.

Thy. Esteem me yet more bitter
    Than crow's-foot evermore,
Rougher than gorse, and viler
    Than seaweed cast ashore,

If this day seem not longer
   To me than all a year :
Go home for shame, ye gluttons,
   Keep me no longer here.

12.

Cor. Oh, ye kind mossy fountains,
   Ye grasses soft as sleep,   90
Ye scanty tufts of arbutus,
   I pray you guard my sheep
Throughout the summer solstice ;
   For lo, the summer'is here,
And summer shoots are sprouting,
   The vine's fresh buds appear.

13.

Thy. Our hearth is primed with fir-cones,
   And piled with blazing oak,
And see—the fire-dogs blackened
   With never-failing smoke ;   100
We care no more for north winds
   Than wolves for tale of sheep,
No more than mountain torrents
   Within their beds to keep.

14.

Cor. The junipers in beauty,
   The prickly chestnuts see,
The golden apples scattered
   Beneath each groaning tree ;

All nature now is smiling,
But should Alexis fly   110
From these his native mountains,
The streams would soon run dry.

15.

Thy. The fields are scorched, the herbage
In all the meads is sere,
Bacchus denies the mountains
Their cloak of vines this year ;
But at our Phillid's coming
The groves will sprout again,
And all the dome of heaven
Descend in copious rain.   120

16.

Cor. Alcides loves the poplar,
And Bacchus loves the vine,
Fair Venus loves the myrtle,
And Phœbus—bays are thine ;
But Phillis loves the hazels,
While hazels pleasure her,
I will not choose the myrtle,
Nor yet the bay prefer.

17.

Thy. The ash reigns o'er the forest,
The cedar o'er the lea,   130
The poplar o'er the rivers,
O'er hills the tall fir tree ;

For Lycidas, if only
    He'will be my frequent guest,
Before the ash or cedar
    My choice shall be confessed.

18.

Mel. My well-considered verdict
    Dooms Thyrsis to defeat ;
Thee, Corydon—our Corydon,
    Our laureate—we greet !

ECLOGUE VIII.—Pharmaceutria.

———*o*———

ARGUMENT.

In the first part of this Eclogue, which is imitated from the third Idyll of Theocritus, the shepherd Damon relates how a youthful suitor of the faithless Nisa bewailed her preference for his rival, Mopso. In the second part, derived from Theocritus' second Idyll, Alphesibœo relates how a fair sorceress used sundry incantations to charm Daphnis back to her arms. This beautiful Eclogue is dedicated to Pollio, who about the time it was written, A. U. C. 715, won a triumph by a victory over the Parthians.

Pha. How once Alphesibœo strove
With Damon, and what strains they wove ;
What time the enraptured heifer stood
And hearkened, heedless of her food ;
While listening lynxes were amazed
At all the worthy shepherd phrased ;
And all the streamlets in the glade
From sheer delight their currents stayed :
Yes, 'it is Alphesibœo's Muse,
And Damon's, for our theme we choose ; 10
Tell me, my Pollio, whether now
Thou'art scaling old Timavo's brow,
Or coasting by the Illyrian strand,
If, as I hope, the day's at hand,

The happy day, when I am free
To celebrate thy deeds and thee;
The day when I may loud proclaim
To all the world the well-earned fame
Of those grand tragedies of thine
Which Sophocles might vote divine   20
(Of thy grand dramas, which I wage
Would well beseem the Athenian stage).
In thee my strains begin and end;
Accept their dedication, friend!
Since at thy bidding they were framed,
There 'is no presumption to be blamed,
Should I my ivy wreath display
Amidst thine own triumphant bay.

Scarce from the silver-spangled sky
Chill shades of Night had turned to fly,   30
And still we saw the dew-drops steep
The tender blades, so dear to sheep,
When Damon on his olive leant,
And thus began the tournament.

I.

Dam. Rise, Lucifer ! be pleased, I pray,
To herald us a genial day,
While, flouted by the heartless jilt,
I rail at cruel Nisa's guilt,
And with my latest breath appeal
To outraged deities to heal   40

The wounds of broken faith.   As yet
But little profit I can get
From their late sanction to our pact,
Since they no penalty exact.
Begin, my own sad flute, with me
The plaintive strains of Arcady.

2.

Mount Mænalus, the whispering pine,
The vocal grove, is ever thine;
The loves of shepherds must appear
Familiar to thy well-trained ear,   50
For was not Pan, who first for men
Made vocal reeds, thy denizen ?
Begin, my own sad flute, with me
The plaintive strains of Arcady.

3.

My Nisa now is Mopso's bride !
What may not lovers soon betide ?
Griffins and mares will shortly mate,
And, at no very distant date,
We 'will surely see the timid does
Carousing with the hounds, their foes :   60
Some bran-new torches, Mopso, cleave,
Your bride will be brought home at eve;
Go, bridegroom, haste your nuts to strew
From Æta, Hesperus flies for you.
Begin, my own sad flute, with me
The plaintive strains of Arcady.

4.

Oh, mated with a worthy mate,
Since worthier suitors you could hate,
Since e'en my flute you dare despise,
Nor do my milch goats in your eyes   70
Find favour, and my length of beard,
My shaggy brows are unrevered ;
Too clear it is you disbelieve
That mortals' wrongs the gods aggrieve.
Begin, my own sad flute, with me
The plaintive strains of Arcady.

5.

How well I still remember you
Out gathering apples in the dew,
An infant at your mother's side,
In our own orchard, I your guide ;   .   80
Myself as yet not twelve years old
(As I have often since been told),
Yet tall enough, as oft we found,
To reach small branches from the ground ;
I saw, and, to my sorrow, sighed,
But now I wish I first had died.
Begin, my own sad flute, with me
The plaintive strains of Arcady.

6.

What love is now, full well I wis,
And whereabouts his birthplace is ;   90

No scion of our blood or race :
Upon the rugged hills of Thrace,
There was he born, or it may be
On Tmarus, or on Rhodope,
Or where the Garamantes dwell
(In furthest Libya, nearest hell).
Begin, my own sad flute, with me
The plaintive strains of Arcady.

7.

'Twas cruel love which once imbrued
A mother's hands with infant blood—   100
Her children's blood—altho' it's true
The mother's heart was cruel too.
But was the mother most to blame ?
Or greater far thy infant shame ?
Her blame I'll not extenuate,
Thee, guilty wretch, I loathe and hate.
Begin, my own sad flute, with me
The plaintive strains of Arcady.

8.

What if the wolf should shun the fold,
The oak yield apples all of gold,   110
The alder bear Narcissus flowers,
The tamarisk weep rich amber showers,
The owl pretend with swans to vie,
And Tityrus Orpheus' self defy !

An Orpheus in the groves, at sea
Arion, Dolphin-king, is he.
Begin, my own sweet flute, with me
A plaintive strain of Arcady.

9.

What if the sea should rage and swell,
And whelm us all: ye woods, farewell !   120
From some high cliff I down will spring,
And headlong in the breakers fling
My broken heart—this legacy
A dying man bequeaths to thee.
Cease now, my own sad lute, with me
The plaintive strains of Arcady.

So Damon sang—come, Muses, say
What next Alphesibœo's lay?
Without your aid we could not sing,
We cannot all do everything.   130

1.

Alp. Come bring us water, and around
These altars be a fillet bound,
And burn some sweet verbenas here,
And frankincense, to mortals dear,
That I by magic rites may try
My spouse's mind to modify.
The charms are ready—there I vow
That only rhymes are missing now

Ye potent spells my efforts crown,
And fetch me Daphnis home from town.　140

2.

Such spells can do their work on high,
And move the moon from out the sky ;
Circe transformed Ulysses' crew
By the magic spells she knew;
A potent spell avails to break
The backbone of the frigid snake.
Ye potent spells my efforts crown,
And fetch me Daphnis home from town.

3.

These threads, all three of diverse dye,
Around this sacred form I tie ;　　　　150
And thrice around these altars draw
The holy image—such the law—
It must be thrice to work aright,
Odd numbers all the powers delight.
Ye potent spells my efforts crown,
And fetch me Daphnis home from town.

4.

Take, Amaryllis, my advice,
And knot the triple colours thrice,
And while you knot them, mind you cry,
" The knots of Venus, lo ! I tie."　　　160

Ye potent spells my efforts crown,
And fetch me Daphnis home from town.

5.

As this clay hardens, and this wax
Doth at the self-same fire relax
Its firm cohesion,—even so,
Let Daphnis when my love 'is aglow ;
Now sprinkle meal, and light me then
The twigs of bay with bitumen ;
As cruel Daphnis burns my heart,
Ye burning bays make Daphnis smart ;   170
Ye potent spells my efforts crown,
And fetch me Daphnis home from town.

6.

Such love for Daphnis I would choose
As hers—the heifer, who pursues
With weary steps the recreant steer,
Thro' groves and thickets far and near,
Till lost at last, beside a brook
She crouches in some sedgy nook,
And when night gathers, sick at heart,
Makes not an effort to depart ;   180
Such love as this may Daphnis feel,
Such love I would not care to heal.
Ye potent spells my efforts crown,
And fetch me Daphnis home from town.

F 2

7.

These keepsakes once, perfidious man,
He left me, when away he ran,
Dear pledges of his love to me,
But now beneath my threshold, see,
I 'will soon commit them to the earth,
Daphnis shall know what they are worth. 190
Ye potent spells my efforts crown,
And fetch me Daphnis home from town.

8.

These herbs—these poisons, all for me,
Were gathered by the Euxine Sea,
Full many by the Euxine grow,
'It was Mœris gave them us, you know ;
I 'have seen him often cross the leas,
A wolf at will, transformed by these.
I 'have seen him often raise the ghosts
From out the sepulchres in hosts, 200
And charm his neighbour's crops with ease
Into his private granaries.
Ye potent spells my efforts crown,
And fetch me Daphnis home from town.

9.

These ashes, Amaryllis, now
Take out of doors, and mind you throw

Them o'er your head into the brook,
And pray be careful not to look ;
Daphnis with these I 'will now assail
Since other spells and philtres fail.   210
Ye potent spells my efforts crown,
And bring me Daphnis home from town.

10.

Look there, while I too long delay
To take the glowing ash away,
The flickering flames themselves have caught
The altars—may it bode us nought
But what is good.   What's that ? but hark !
Did Hylax at the threshold bark ?
I dreamed, but then, alas, it 'is plain
That those who love oft dream in vain.   220
Come, lay your spells and philtres down,
Here 'is Daphnis now, come home from town.

ECLOGUE IX.—Mœris.

———o———

ARGUMENT.

When the military colonists, referred to in the first Eclogue, took possession of the lands assigned them at Mantua and Cremona, it is related that Virgil was subjected to some rough usage by the Centurion, Arius, who was to be the new proprietor of his confiscated acres, and only saved his life by a swim across the Mincio. He thereupon started for Rome to obtain redress from Octavian, leaving his steward, Mœris, at home, with instructions to propitiate the intruder by soft words and polite attentions. The opening scene of this Eclogue exhibits Mœris on his way into Mantua with presents for his foe, and engaged in conversation with his friend, Lycidas, whom he has met, on the fortunes of the Poet under the pseudonym of Menalcas.

Lycidas.

Is it to town that Mœris speeds?
To Mantua that highway leads.

Mœris.

Ah, Lycidas, to our dismay
We have lived to see the evil day
We little thought to see; and hear,
What we had never learnt to fear,

An alien Lord's ejectment writ,
"These lands are mine, old Tenants quit!"
And we, poor victims, forth must go,
Since Fortune turns the tables so ;   10
These kids of ours we send him now
With no good wishes, I avow.

Lycidas.

Your tidings fill me with surprise,
For I had certainly been told
    That your Menalcas, void of wrongs,
    Had saved his acres by his songs.
Permitted still his lands to hold,
    That pretty farm of his that lies
Just where the bluffs, no longer bold,
    Fall off in gentle slopes, that sink   20
    To where those veteran beeches grow,
    Whose age their battered branches show,
        Beside the Mincio's brink.

Mœris.

No doubt, for so the rumour ran ;
But our songs, Lycidas, my man,
Among the rampant soldiers here
Are worth about as much, I fear,
As cooings, where the eagle roves,
To doves that haunt Chaonian groves :
For if the raven's boding croak,   30
Resounding from the hollow oak,

Had failed to warn us, at all cost,
Conciliation to exhaust,
No Mœris here alive you'd see;
Menalcas with the shades would be.

Lycidas.

.   Ah! I could scarcely have believed
Such wickedness had been conceived!
And we 'have so nearly been deprived
Of you, and all the joys derived
From your sweet lays, Menalcas! who   40
But you, would sing of nymphs, and strew
The land with flowers? or laud the shade
Where fountains bubble in the glade?
Such lays as late by stealth I heard
Low-read—and drank in every word.
'It was at our Amaryllid's—whom
You went to visit—in her room—
"Oh Tityrus, till I come back
I pray you see my milch goats lack
Nor food nor water—short the way,   50
'It is not my purpose to delay,
But while you tend them have a care,—
The old goat butts—so pray beware!"

Mœris.

Or such as these unfinished lines
Which he for Varus now designs—

" Oh, Varus, if but Mantua still
Be left to us your friends to till,
Our Mantua—alas, too near
To poor Cremona, much I fear,—
The swans shall bear your name on high,   60
And hymn your praises to the sky."

Lycidas.

Come now—so may your swarms eschew
The poisonous flowers of the yew,
So may the Cytisus befriend
Your heifers and their dugs distend.
Begin, and let us hear you sing,
And make the woods with music ring.
A bard am I,—I 'have written lays—
And shepherds oft my powers praise
(But some, maybe, would praise the crows). 70
On me no flatterers impose,
For nothing in my songs I find
Worthy of Cinna, to my mind,
Or Varus, nay, I only seem
A goose, among the swans to scream.

Mœris.

I do as much—and, all this while,
My seeming silence I beguile
In striving to recall one, lad,
I have it now—it 'is not so bad.

He sings.

" What pleasure is there on the waves   80
Whose perils Galatea braves?
Come hither, maid, the gorgeous spring
In beauty mantles every thing :
She clothes the spangled ground with flowers,
The clambering vine festoons the bowers,
The poplar quivers o'er the cave,
Its threshold running waters lave ;
Come hither, then, and mind no more
The wild waves dashing on the shore."

Lycidas.

One starlight night I heard a song   90
By gentle zephyrs borne along.
What was it?   Well I knew the tune,
The words escaped me all too soon.

Maris.

" Oh, Daphnis, why in rapt surprise
Watch ancient constellations rise?
'It is Cæsar's constellation now
Should occupy your thoughts, I trow,
His star which raises harvest hopes
And tints the grape on sunny slopes.
Come, Daphnis, graft your pears, their fruit 100
Will haply be your grandson's loot."
Age robs us all of everything,
And memory itself takes wing.

How often, when myself a boy,
Long days in music I'd employ;
Now half my songs have left my head,
My very voice itself has fled.
And why?—before I chanced to see
The wolf, the vagabond saw me!
Let that suffice; Menalcas soon   110
Will sing the whole in better tune.

Lycidas.

Our mouths but water all the more
For all the excuses that you pour!
Now all the broad expanse of lake
Is smooth and silent for your sake,
The whispering winds are hushed and still,
And we have reached our half-way hill;
For now I see Bianor's tomb
O'ershadowed by the thicket's gloom,
Where oft the peasants lop the boughs—   120
A spot well suited to our vows;
Let 'us put the kids down here, and sing;
We 'will reach the town ere evening:
Or, if we should have cause for fear
That night will gather rain-clouds here,
Why let us then indulge in song,
As cheerily we march along,
So best our journey we 'will beguile;
I 'will ease you of your load the while.

Mœris.

No more, my lads, let's mind our business
   now,   130
We'll sing much better when he comes, I
   trow.

ECLOGUE X.—GALLUS.

——o——

ARGUMENT.

This Eclogue, a love lay, which owes a great deal to the first Idyll of Theocritus, appears to have been written at the request of Gallus, a favourite lieutenant of Octavian, on the subject of his luckless love affairs with the Actress Cytheris, under the pseudonym of Lycoris. Gallus is represented as driven by his despair into Arcadia, where his friends, human and divine, assemble to console him. [The end of Gallus was unfortunate. He was made Governor of Egypt, and it is related of him that during his term of office he destroyed Thebes. He was spoiled by prosperity, and finally showed a rebellious spirit towards his benefactor, was disgraced, and destroyed himself; but was, nevertheless, much lamented by his Imperial friend.]

DEIGN, Arethusa, what I ask,
To undertake—but one more task.
So, when beneath Sicilian brine
Thou flowest—shall it ne'er be thine
To mingle with the bitter waves
That sea-nymphs brew in ocean caves;
For still to me it now remains
To sing for Gallus some few strains,

And, if Lycoris read them, well !
Let Gallus freely use their spell !   10
Come then, begin, for I propose
The loves of Gallus to disclose !
Our dainty goats will browse the while
The tender shrubs and camomile—
Nature 'is not deaf to whom we sing,
We 'will make the echoing woodlands ring.
What were the groves, and what the glades,
Which so detained ye, thoughtless maids ?
Ye Naïads, while to love resigned—
Unworthy love—our Gallus pined.   20
'It was not by Pindus, I 'am assured,
Nor yet Parnassus, so allured, ·
Nor Aganippe's crystal fount
That wells from out the Aonian mount.
Why, e'ven the bays bemoaned his lot,
That Tamarisks wept I marvel not,
And Mænalus, with all its pines,
For he had sought its lonely shrines,
And all the many ice-clad stones
Which snow-capped mount Lycæus   30
    owns ;
Aye, as he lay beneath the rocks
There gathered round him all the flocks :
The gentle sheep would not despise
Their shepherd ; wherefore, in your eyes,
Great Poet, should they seem so vile ?
Adonis led them many a mile.

The shepherds too came ; then at last,
The cowherds—never over fast.
Menalcas then, drenched through and
    through
From gathering acorns in the dew.   40
One query one and all propose,
" Whence that delirious passion flows ? "
Apollo in his turn inquires
" What phrensy now your soul inspires ?
Lycoris for another swain
Braves realms of snow and frozen rain."
Sylvanus, next in turn, comes round,
His head with rustic honours crowned,
With tiger-lilies for a brand,
And fennel-flowers in his hand.   50
Pan next, the Arcadian god appeared,
We saw him with his face besmeared
With crimson elderberry juice,
And eke vermilion dyes profuse,
And he the same demand propounds—
·" What ! has this passion then no bounds ?
Think not fell love can so be eased,
Nor with such glut of tears appeased.
I know not who 'ever sated sees
With brooks the meads, with trefoil bees."   60
But he, still sick at heart, replied :
" Ye kind Arcadians, I confide
In you to make your mountains ring,
And sing as none but you can sing

My sorrows : then my bones will lie
In mother earth, how tranquilly !
Then let your vocal reeds all tell
How I have loved so long, so well.
I would that I had erst been born
As one of you, and ne'ver been torn   70
From my own native shepherd's cot,
Or some ancestral vine-clad spot ;
For Phyllis then, as I opine,
Or else Amyntas had been mine,
Or else some other flame as dear
(And what if good Amyntas here
Be dusky, are not violets dark,
And hyacinths—both flowers of mark ?)
Then by the olive or the vine,
My love with me would oft recline.   80
Then Phyllis would my chaplets tie,
Amyntas warble cheerily—
Here all the crystal founts are cool,
Soft meadows here surround each pool,
And grove—here, sweet Lycoris, too,
How happy could I be with you,
And spend my life so void of care,
That nought but time my frame would
        wear.
Now cruel Mars my homage claims,
And to the camp my fortune chains,   90
While in the midst of arms and foes,
I suffer passion's phrensied throes ;

And you, the while, afar from home,
I scarce believe it,—lonely roam
Amidst the cruel Alpine snows,
Or Rhenish frosts may be—who knows?
Oh! may the frosts not harm thee, sweet,
Or rough ice cut thy tender feet.
Well, now, methinks, that I'll rehearse
My treasure of Euboeic verse   100
The while my reed in concert dares
The old Sicilian shepherd's airs.
Ah, well I know I 'would rather brood
Upon my woes in solitude,
Among the savage wild beasts' dens,
Among the thickets in the glens,
And carve my tale of love at ease
Upon the tender bark of trees;
So carved that with their growth 'it would
     grow.
But now among the nymphs I 'will go   110
To Mænalus, and ramble o'er
His rugged crags, or hunt the boar.
No snows shall stop, no frosts shall stay
My ardour for the hunt to-day:
My rattling hounds shall make their raid
Upon each wild Parthenian glade:
Already now my spirit roves
Among the rocks and ringing groves;
Already now I seem to throw
The Cretan dart from Parthian bow: 120

G

As if such remedies could cure
The phrensy that I now endure!
As if the God of love aye thrills
With pity for our human ills!
So now of these delights I tire,
And not the lays that ye inspire
O, Hamadryads! can appease
My pains—no more the woodlands please;
How far so 'ever our art may range,
The course of love we cannot change.   130
Not should we, half frost-bitten, drink
At Thracian Hebro's frozen brink, ·
Or, in mid-winter, undergo
The horrors of Sithonian snow.
Not if we led our sheep to graze
Beneath the tropics, where the rays
Of Nubian suns, (God save the mark),
Would scorch the tall elms' inner bark.
Triumphant love is lord of all,
Then let us at his footstool fall.   140

  Suffice it, muses, that your bard
Should sing thus far, upon the sward
The while he sits, and nimbly plaits
With supple flag the basket mats.
And now we pray that ye will cause
Gallus to hear him with applause:
Gallus, for whom our love still grows
From hour to hour, as each day shows,

As fast as alders, when in spring
Their early shoots are lengthening.   150
Come, let us rise, for evening shade
May harm the minstrel in the glade.
Of shade the crops at times complain,
And deem it baneful to the grain ;
Hie homeward, goats, hie, gluttons, hie,
There 'is Hesperus rising in the sky.

ODES *of* HORACE.

INDEX.

TO THE SHIP WHICH WAS TO TAKE VIRGIL TO
ATHENS.

Sic te diva potens Cypri.

I PRAY the Cyprian goddess queen,
    And Helen's twin kin-stars of glorious sheen,
I pray the parent of the gales
    Protect thee, by withholding from thy sails
All but the breeze which eastward blows,
    If thou, O! ship, in answer to my vows,
Wilt only, as is meet, restore
    Our Virgil safely to the Attic shore,
And so preserve full half my soul,
    Entrusted for the nonce to thy control.   10
Breastplate of brass in triple fold
    He surely wore, who whilom was so bold,
As first of men to venture to consign
    His fragile pinnace to the ruthless brine;
Nor held in awe the fearful shock
    Of Boreas wrestling with the dread Siroc;
Nor yet the Hyads, boding rain,
    Nor yet the wild South-wester's hurricane,

Who, sternest lord that Hadria knows,
 Calls her sea-waves to anger or repose. 20
What form of death could he have feared,
 To whose unshrinking eye there first appeared
The monsters of the deep? who first
 Saw the seas lash Keraunian cliffs accursed?
Jove's caution purposed, all in vain,
 To part the earth for ever from the main
If impious rafts persistently
 Will dare to trespass on the holy sea.
Mankind is ever prone to dare
 All dangers, and in paths forbidden fare. 30
The daring once of Japhet's race
 Abstracted fire from out the realms of space :
When fire was first brought down to earth,
 A brood of ghastly evils had their birth !
Consumption then, and fevers dire
 Provoked his tardy hand to swifter ire,
And quickened then death's lagging pace—
 Then Dædalus essayed to traverse space
On pinions never meant for man,
 The toils of Hercules attained to span 40
The floods of Acheron—what then !
 There is nothing left too arduous for men !
Our folly even soars so high,
 That we aspire to scale the very sky,
Nor will our wild and wicked pride
 Let Jove's hand lay his bolts of wrath aside.

LIB. I. ODE V.

TO PYRRHA.

Quis multâ gracilis te puer in rosâ.

1.

OH, who is the stripling so scented and slim,
Who now in your pleasant grot, Pyrrha, reposes
On litter of roses,
Still cooing and wooing?
Those tresses of gold you have braided for him,

2.

With charming simplicity! ere very long,
For all he is now so confiding a lover,
He 'will surely discover
Sad treason in season,
The smooth waters ruffled by breezes so strong.

3.

Fond fool! he believes you as sterling as gold,
And trusts he will find you for ever as tender,
As prone to surrender;
Not ruing what's brewing,
Alas! for the wights who 'have not known thee of
old.

4.

The walls of the temple bear witness for me,
Who hung up my raiment just after one dipping,
    All soaking and dripping ;
    My motive was votive ;
My thanks they were due to the God of the Sea.

Lib. I. Ode IX.

TO THALIARCH.

Vides ut altâ stet nive candidum.

See how Soracte's towering crest
    Gleams white with snow, and the laden trees
How they creak and groan with the weight
      oppressed!
    See how the torrents freeze!

Consume the cold! here, logs of pine—
    Come, heap up the hearth with good dry
      wood!
Bring up, if you please, the Sabine wine,
    The four-year old—the good!

Leave all the rest to heaven, for when
    The Gods have allayed the fierce Siroc   10
That wars with the waves, no cypress then,
    Or mountain ash will rock.

Seek not to dip in the well of time,
    Each day that the fates accord, set down
As so much gain, nor in youth's glad prime
    Despise sweet love, nor frown

Upon the dance while the sap is green,
    And surly age keeps aloof ; but now
For sports and pastimes, sweet seventeen,
    The twilight-whispered vow,—   20

The tell-tale laugh of the girl we love,
    From the nook she has made her lair—
Come, wrest from her hand a scarf or glove,
    In spite of her feigned " forbear."

LIB. I. ODE XI.

TO LEUCONOE.

Tu ne quæsieris.

WHAT the term of days awarded
   By the Gods to thee—to me,
Ask not ! it is forbidden knowledge
   Banned of heaven, Leuconoe.
Question not the magic tables
   Of the Babylonian seer,
Better brave whate'er may happen,
   Whether Jove designs us here
Many winters, or has destined
   This to be our very last,   10
This, which wastes the Tuscan billows
   By the fury of its blast.
Come, be wise, and let the vintage
   Melt the mellow grape to wine,
Brief as is the destined season,
   Length of hope must not be thine.
Even now, while we are speaking,
   Time impatient flits away ;
Trust but little to to-morrow,
   Make the utmost of to-day   20

THE PROPHECY OF NEREUS.

Pastor cum traheret.

When the shepherd prince was taking
  Ravished Helen o'er the seas,
Treacherously seized and borne in
  Phrygian bark to Trojan leas,
Father Nereus left the swift winds,
  Left them to unwonted ease
While he sang the awful burden
  Of their hidden destinies.

Evil omens—thus he chanted,
  Evil omens tend the bride,   10
Whom united Greece will follow—
  Follow up with all her pride,
Sworn to break the fatal nuptials.
  Priam's ancient throne beside.

Sorry work for horse and rider,
　Sorry work for son and sire.
Ah ! what mourning you will cause by
　Many a sad Dardanian pyre ;
Pallas now prepares her ægis,
　Helm, and car, with reckless ire.　　　　20

All in vain you comb those tresses,
　Fondly trusting Venus' aids ;
All in vain you touch those harp-strings,
　Striking chords erst left for maids ;
Softest couches will not shield you—
　Shield you from the Grecian blades.

Surely 'it is not so you purpose
　Shunning winged Cretan bows,
Shunning all the din of battle,
　Ajax fleetest of your foes,—　　　　30
Vainly ! that vile head is destined,—
　None too soon,—to feed the crows.

See you not Laertes' offspring !
　Bane of your devoted race ?
See you not the honoured Nestor ?
　Teucer, too, whom you must face ?
Salamis will find him for you,
　Warrior of unequalled grace.

See you not that matchless soldier,
  Sthenelus, so skilled to tame   40
Fiery steeds ; and noble Meryon ?
  Well, methinks, you know his name !
See, Tydides burns to find you,
  Born to dim his father's fame.

Like a frightened stag you'will flee him,
  Stag that hears the baying hound,
And, unmindful of his grazing,
  Spurns the turf with lightest bound.
Panting with a craven sighing,—
  Was it thus your bride was found ?   50

See, it comes, the day of reckoning,
  Grecian fleet to Ilion's strand,
Woe betiding Phrygian matrons,
  Woe betiding Phrygian land.
Not many winters more, and then,—
  Trojan homes for Grecian brand !

NOTE.— This Ode was translated at sea, in sight of the Plains
of Troy, in July, 1864.

TO CHLOE.

Vitas hinnuleo.

1.

CHLOE! CHLOE ! wherefore fly
Like a filly, young and shy,—
Seeking a'mid the maze of hills
Its frightened dam,—whom panic thrills,
At every breeze that stirs the trees?

2.

When winds whispering "spring is nigh"
Through the rustling leaflets sigh ;
When bright green lizards as they glide
Just push the tangled brakes aside;
See! how heart-tremor shakes her knees.   10

3.

No fierce tiger, puss, am I,
No wild lion who would try
To eat you up! Then wherefore flee?
Come, leave your mother's side for me—
A woman now, and born to please !

H

LIB. I.   ODE XXXVII.

TO HIS BOON COMPANIONS.

Nunc est bibendum.

Now fill your glasses, now foot it merrily,
Strike up the galop, now for your banquetings,
   Now deck the Gods' shrines with your gar-
      lands,
   Now is the time for your fêtes, my comrades.

Not one day sooner were you at liberty
Out of the cherished bins of your ancestors,
   To drink the choice wines, while the mad
      queen
   Plotted the downfall of Roman grandeur.

With all her vile suite, nourished in infamy,
Perished with riot, was there a hope for her?   10
   What tho' she was drunk with good fortune,
   Soon she had need to restrain her phrensy.

Scarce of her whole fleet was there a vessel left,
Such conflagration !—Cæsar was terrible.
    He taught her, though wine-drenched, what
        fear was,
    When in a panic he drove her homewards,

Plying his oars well—just as a sparrow-hawk
Chases a ringdove, or as the harriers
    Hunt down the poor hare in the lowlands,
    White with the flakes of the driving snow-
        storm.   20

He would have chained his mischievous enemy,
She dared to choose death rather than misery ;
    She had no woman's fear of cold steel ;
    She would not hide with her fleet in corners.

She dared re-seek her desolate palaces :
Calm on her brave face, she could manipulate
    Rude asps without flinching, and welcome
    Venomous fangs on her splendid bosom.

In her determined death more invincible
Than Cæsar's wild Liburnian savages ;   30
    Her woman's pride never could stoop to
    Dangle her chains in the victor's triumph !

Lib. I. Ode XXXVIII.

TO HIS SERVING MAN.

Persicos odi, puer, apparatus.

1.

THE gay gauds of Persia, I hate them, my lad,
　And ribanded wreaths I'd rather not see ;
Why search if there 'is still a late rose to be had ?
　The last rose of summer is nothing to me.

2.

Mere myrtle is ample for all that I care,
　Pray mingle nought else with that myrtle of
　　mine ;
It is not too fine for a flunkey to wear,
　Or his wine-bibbing liege in his arbour of vine.

TO DELIUS.

Æquam memento rebus in arduis.

1.

In adversity remember
    To preserve an even mind,
So in prosperous days your spirits
    In due bounds will be confined,
Free from arrogance, my friend,
Not unmindful of your end.

2.

Whether all your life is sadness,
    Or at ease, on some green knoll,
Through long days of endless revel
    You have comforted your soul   10
With Falernian, from the bin
Of your favourite brand within.

3.

Where huge pines and hoary poplars
    Love to weave a grateful shade,
Waving welcome with their branches,
    While the streamlet in the glade
Winding, delving through the soil,
Seems to tremble with its toil.

4.

Thither with the wine and perfumes,
    Bid them bring the sweet frail rose,   20
While as yet on youth fair fortune
    All its choicest gifts bestows,
And the sisters that we dread
Leave uncut the triple thread.

5.

You must leave your purchased forest,
    You must leave your mountain home,
You must leave your villa, watered
    By the Tiber's yellow foam ;
And some reckless heir will spend
Heaps of wealth you loved to tend.   30

6.

Whether you are born a Dives,
    With an ancient pedigree,
Little matters, or a pauper
    Living 'neath the open sky ;

Ruthless fate will have its way !
You must be the spoiler's prey !

7.

One sure road we all must travel,
   For us all there is an urn,
Which one day must be inverted,
   And our lot be drawn in turn :   40
O'er the ferry to be sent
To eternal banishment !

LIB. II. ODE X.

TO LICINIUS.

Rectius vives, Licini, neque altum.

My rule of life, Licinius, hear !
    Tempt not for aye the open sea ;
Nor yet, through dread of tempests, steer
    Too close beside the rock-bound lee.
Whoever loves the golden mean,
    Will keep his roof in good repair,
Too simple in his tastes, I ween,
    For modern modes to care.

The largest pine in wintry squalls
    Most often rocks ; with heaviest crash   10
The tallest turret ever falls :
    High peaks attract the lightning's flash.
With hope, when fortune favours not,
    When fortune smiles, why, then with fear
The well-trained mind regards its lot,
    For Jupiter is near ;

Who, after winter, sends us springs.
  Do not our troubles come and go ?
Apollo takes his harp and sings,—
  And does not always bend his bow.   20
What, if your means are narrow ;—wear
  A dauntless face, and never quail,
But if the gales blow fresh and fair,
  Be wise, and shorten sail.

LIB. II. ODE XIII.

TO A FALLING TREE.

Ille et nefasto te posuit die.

1.

IT was a luckless day, O tree,
When he—whoever planted thee
First set thee out, with impious hand,
To be the by-word of the land,
    The bane of his own progeny.

2.

I could believe that fellow broke
His father's neck, and stained the oak
Of his own inner chamber floor
With his confiding guest's sprent gore,
    And dealt in venoms with the folk   10

3.

Of Colchis ; ay and foremost led
What villanies were ever bred ;
Who set thee in this field of mine,
To fall one day, O log malign,
    Upon my harmless head.

4.

To shun what hourly dangers need
Most caution, men take little heed ;
The mariners of Carthage hate
The Bosphorus, heedless if swift fate
    From other source proceed.   20

5.

Reluctantly the soldier dares
The flying Parthian, who forswears
Italian prisons ; but the might
Of death is ever apt to smite
    Its victims unawares.

6.

How very nearly it was mine
To view the realms of Proserpine,
And Æacus upon his seat
Of judgment, and the sure retreat,
    Where shades in bliss recline :   30

7.

Where Sappho sweeps her plaintive strings,
And of her favoured sisters sings ;
While perils of the sea, and eke
The woes of war, and exile, wake
    Alcæo's grander carollings.

8.

With sacred silence, as is right,
The listening shades the twain requite ;
But tales of tyrants overthrown,
And martial strains do most, I own,
  The thronging crowds delight.   40

9.

What wonder !—when, beneath their spell,
The hundred-headed hound of hell
Droops his black ears ; and pleasure wakes
Contortions in the coil of snakes
  That wreathe the locks of Furies fell.

10.

Prometheus also, and the sire
Of Pelops, feel their labour dire
Beguiled by those harmonious airs :
Orion's self no longer cares
  For timid lynx, or lion's ire.   50

Lib. II. Ode XIV.

TO POSTHUMUS.

Eheu fugaces, Postume, Postume.

1.

Fleeting, oh ! how swiftly fleeting,
  Speed the rolling years away !
Virtue will not smooth the wrinkles,
Will not thaw the snow that sprinkles
    Locks of eld, nor serve to stay
    Death's approaches for a day.

2.

No, my friend, if thrice a hundred
  Bulls were daily sacrificed,
On the red and reeking altars
Of the God who never falters,   10
    Nor relaxes his firm hold
    On the mighty men of old.

3.

Thou wouldst not appease his craving;
  All the souls that people earth,
Whatsoever their condition,
Whether peasant or patrician,
    Must at length, by sure decree,
    Sail across his gloomy sea.

4.

Vainly shall we shirk the perils
  Of the ocean and the land ;   20
Vainly shun the fields of battle,
Or the rocks where tempests rattle ;
    Vainly take a timely flight,
    From the East wind and the blight.

5.

We must visit black Cocytus,
  Flowing with its languid stream ;
We must go where Danaus' daughters
Expiate those fearful slaughters ;
    Where his task, in shadowy guise,
    Sisyphus for ever plies.   30

6.

We must leave both wife and children,
  We must leave both house and home ;
None, of all thy pet plantation,
Coaxed by careful cultivation,
    Save the hated cypress tree
    Shall attend its brief lessee.

7.

Some more worthy heir will revel
  In the choicest stoups of wine,
In thy secret cellar hoarded :
And, with liqueurs not accorded   40
    To the Pontiff's pampered suite,
    Stain the pavement at his feet.

THE VANITY OF LUXURY.

Non ebur neque aureum.

In my home no gilded ceilings
   Gleam on ivory and gold,
No columns hewn in Libyan quarries
   Beams of polished oak uphold.
I lord it o'er no miser's palace,
   Like some unknown upstart heir ;
To woo my vote with webs of purple,
   Fawning matrons never care.
But I am trusty, and of humour
   I possess a pleasant vein ;   10
Tho' I'am poor, the rich affect me,
   Wherefore, then, should I complain ?
With continual suits to pester
   Friends in power I'am little prone ;
Quite content among the Sabines,
   With the little farm I own,
So one day succeeds another
   Like the billows on the main,
So my life's calm glamour passes
   While the new moons wax and wane.   20

As for you, you 'are planning mansions,
　　Thoughtless of the yawning tomb,
Sending marbles to the mason,
　　Close upon your day of doom.
On the pleasant Bay of Baiæ
　　Gyves for Neptune you prepare,
Discontented with the limits
　　That his shores have set you there.
Must you move your neighbour's land-
　　　marks ?
　　Where will Avarice stay its hand ?　　　30
Must you trespass on the borders
　　Of your humble tenant's land ?
Drive him forth with his Penates,
　　Wildly clasping to his breast
Weeping wife and squalid children,
　　(At his wits' end where to rest ?)
Yet no palace is more surely
　　Trimmed for Dives, at the last,
Than the bourne of ravening Orcus,
　　When his lease of life is past.　　　40
Earth, impartial, bares her bosom,—
　　Whither then extends your aim ?—
As for peasants, so for princes ;
　　Meting out to all the same.
Hell would not release Prometheus,
　　Nor its Usher take a bribe ;
He it is who curbs the miser,
　　And the miser's hated tribe ;

He it is who frees the pauper,
   When his life-long toil is o'er ;   50
He it is who comes when summoned,—
   Comes unsummoned—to the door !

———*o*———

Lib. III. Ode II.

TO THE ROMANS.

Angustam, amici, pauperiem pati.

I.

In the school of active warfare
   Let thy boy, my friend, be reared,
To endure good sharp privation,
   As a trooper to be feared ;
Let him check the foe's advance
With the terror of his lance.

2.

Let him rough it in the open,
   Let him live in war's alarms,
So that when, from walls beleaguered,
   Royal ladies flaunt their charms,   10
He may catch the matron's eye,
While the daughter, with a sigh,

I

3.

Whispers, " May my precious husband,
　　Deeds of war unused to dare,
Never venture to encounter
　　That fierce lion in his lair,
Whom such fury doth impel
Thro' the bloody jaws of hell."

4.

Oh, how sweet it is, and glorious,
　　For one's fatherland to die !   20
Death pursues the flying coward,
　　Harmless youth 'it will not pass by,
Tho' his timid knees should quake,
Tho' his back a target make.

5.

Valour, petty buffets scorning,
　　Wears its gold without a stain,
Will not raise or sink its standard;
　　Will not bate its proud disdain,
At the bidding of the crowd,
Tho' its voice be raised aloud.   30

6.

Valour, opening heaven's portals
　　For the men who should not die,
Strives to travel paths forbidden
　　To the regions of the sky;

Spurning, like a strong-winged bird,
Earth, and all the vulgar herd.

7.

And, moreover, sound discretion
　Wins its own assured reward ;
He who blabs the rites of Ceres
　Shall not share my sacred board ;　　40
Nor his frail bark put to sea,
If I have my will, with me.

8.

Heaven hath often, in one ruin,
　To avenge its slighted shrine,
Overwhelmed both saint and sinner
　In a flood of wrath divine :
Justice, tho' it seem to halt,
Rarely will be found at fault.

Lib. III.   Ode III.

THE EFFICACY OF VIRTUE AND RESOLUTION.

Justum et tenacem propositi virum.

1.

One of determined purpose and honesty
  No, not the wrath of wrong-headed citizens,
  No, nor the tyrant's frowning visage,
Turns from his purpose aside; no storm wind,

2.

Reigning resistless, mistress of Adria;
  No, nor Jove's right hand wielding the thunder-
    bolt:
If all around him fell the crushed globe,
Fearless he 'would perish among the ruins.

3.

'Twas thus did Pollux, thus the great Hercules,
  Ascend the glowing heights of the firmament,   10
  Twixt whom the great Cæsar, reclining,
Sips with his roseate lips the nectar.

4.

Thus was it, Bacchus, thy lot of Tiger whelps
  Learnt to submit their necks to the collar
    strap,
Untamed aforetime : so Quirinus
'Scaped Acheron with the steeds of Mavors.

5.

Welcome the speech that Juno pronounced before
  The Gods in Council. Ilion, Ilion,
  That dissolute damned arbiter, that
Frailest of foreigners, overthrew thee,—   20

6.

Laid thee low-lying ; ay, when Laomedon
Forswore his pledged words,—cheated the Gods
    above,—
  Then, with thy false king and thy people,
Doomed both by me and by chaste Minerva.

7.

No more the splendid Spartan adulteress,
Nor her seducer, reigns in impunity,
  Nor does the perjured house of Priam
Brave my good Greeks by the might of Hector.

8.

No more the conflict through our Olympian
Strife is protracted.   Time I should yield to
    Mars   30
  My wrath, and his hated descendant,
Born of the Priestess of Troy's High Altar.

9.

Him, of my free grace, I will admit to the
Mansions celestial, not without liberty
    To quaff the rich nectar, and write his
      Name on the rolls of the Gods Olympic.

10.

So long the salt waves roll between Ilion
And distant Rome, so long let the exiles reign
  Uncursed in what home they 'have adopted,
If but the cattle range unmolested,   40

11.

And hateful wild beasts kennel their progeny
On those dishonoured bones of their ancestors ;
  While Rome gives her laws to the wide world,
And her proud Capitol stands in splendour.

12.

So let her name be feared to the uttermost
Corner of earth's bounds, where the mid ocean
  Divideth our Europe from Afric,
Where the rich corn-levels hail the Nile flood,

13.

Strong in her scorn of gold—yet invisible,—
Gold, which were better down in the mine below, 50
   Than won for the service of mortals
By sacrilegious and reckless robbers.

14.

Yes! whatsoever shores be earth's boundaries,
Her arms shall reach them, all undeterred by the
   Fierce shocks of convulsions volcanic,
Or the damp mists of eternal showers.

15.

This only caution, mandate of destiny,
Bind those Quirites :—let not their piety,
   Confiding in fortune's caresses,
Dare to repair the old walls of Priam. 60

16.

Phœnix-like else will Troy's evil genius,
Hungering for slaughter, shake his foul pinions,
   Myself, Jove's sister-wife, relentless,
Heading the hosts of avenging armies.

17.

Thrice if her walls rose, forged in the brass furnace,
By Phœbus's own hands, thrice should they levelled
   be,—
   Razed by my Argives ; thrice her widows—
Mourn in captivity all their slain sons.

18.

Ah ! these are strains too sad for my minstrelsy ;
Whither, oh ! wayward Muse, art thou wander-
    ing?   70
  The Speech of Immortals befits not
  Melodies never yet tuned for grand themes.

———o———

LIB. III.   ODE XIX.

TO TELEPHUS.

Quantum distet ab Inacho.

You tell us, no doubt it is perfectly true,
  How long after Inachus Codrus came,
Of his death and about the Æacidæ too,
  And what were the wars which set Troy in
    a flame.
It is all very well, but what has it to do
With the price of a cask of old Chian ? or who
Shall heat us the water, and make the brew
  boil,
When we are quite fagged with pedestrian toil
Up there on the Apennines? nor have you
  said
Who 'will ask us to dinner, or find us a bed.   10

Come, fill up your glasses, and drink to the
      moon,
And drink to the cock-crow! what, drained
      them so soon ?
Then toast the new Augur, Muræna, for he
Must receive all the honours,—thrice-over the
      three.
Yes, the priest of the Muses who frequently
      feels
Their divine inspiration which over him steals,
Could not put up with less than thrice-over
      the three :
The graces, fair girls, with their charms so
      free,
Fear a breach of the peace, and would only
      have three.
But it is good to be daft, just for once in a way : 20
Then, oh ! why should the fife be silent to-day ?
And wherefore, oh wherefore, now hang up the
      lyre ?
A fig for the fingers that know how to tire :
Come, shower the roses, and never you fear
If Lycus, old churl, our revels should hear ;
I'll be bound it is envy he 'will feel to the core,
And his ill-mated leman will feel it yet more.
Oh ! Telephus, Rhoda, the rosebud of girls,
    Just out in the world, why, she runs after you,
She has fallen in love with your glossy black
      curls ;   30

And dreams you so handsome, so spruce,
    and so true,
As bright and as pure as the star of the Eve !
Your triumphs it is not for me to achieve ;
My love is consuming me slowly, you see,
For Glycera is not so loving to me !

———*o*———

LIB. III.   ODE XXII.

TO DIANA.

Montium Custos.

I.

Oh goddess, guardian of the hill and glade,
Who, thrice invoked, art prompt to lend thine
    aid
To young expectant mothers in their pangs,
And snatch them scatheless from death's cruel
    fangs,
        Diana, triune maid !

2.

Know that henceforth I dedicate to thee
This pine that shades my cottage, noble tree,
A wild boar's blood, slain ere 'it can bestow,
With slanting tusks, the meditated blow,
        Shall be its annual fee.   10

TO VENUS.

Vixi puellis.

1.

I 'HAVE lived a lady's man till now,
  And have not served without repute ;
  But now I have finished with my lute,
I 'will hang up all the kit, I vow,

2.

At Venus' shrine—the left-hand wall ;
  Yes, that's the place,—come now, my lambs,
  Hang there the crowbars, links, and rams
I used to breach the doors withal :

3.

O goddess of the Cyprian isle,
  And Memphis never vexed with snow,   10
  Oh raise thy lash for one smart blow,
And punish Chloe for her guile.

LIB. IV. ODE VII.

TO TORQUATUS.

Diffugêre nives.

1.

GONE are the snows, and the grasses
  Are showing their face on the meadows,
  So are the fronds on the trees.

2.

Earth is renewing her seasons,
The brooks to their banks are withdrawing
  Waters which covered the leas.

3.

Nymphs with the graces are tripping
Away thro' the maze of the dances,
  Careless of hiding their charms.

4.

Time, which makes havoc of pleasure,   10
And seasons forbid us to cherish
  Hopes of immortal delight.

5.

Frosts are expelled by the zephyrs,
The spring is expelled by the summer,
   Destined to die in its turn :

6.

When, with its apples, old autumn
Has gathered the spoils of the harvest,
   Winter is on us again.

7.

Moons may be swift to recover
The losses they suffer in waning,   20
   We, when we fall, like the leaves,

8.

Whither did father Æneas,
And Tullus the monarch, and Ancus,
   Turn into shadow and dust.

9.

Who can say, whether the purpose
Of God is to add an hereafter
   For us to the boon of to-day ?

10.

Heirs cannot easily plunder,
How grasping soever their fingers,
   Gifts thou hast made to thy mind.   30

11.

Once thou art dead, and old Minos
Hath had thee arraigned, and pronounced his
 Last solemn judgment on thee,

12.

Eloquence, virtue, or birthright,
Will serve thee but little thereafter
 To win back thy former degree.

13.

Out of the shadows of Orcus
Not even Diana herself could
 Rescue Hippolyta's son ;

14.

Vain was the prowess of Theseus,   40
When he from the fetters of Lethe
 Sought to deliver his friend.

COUNTRY LIFE.

Beatus ille qui procul negotiis.

How happy is the man who free from busy care,
    As were the primal races of the earth,
Can till his own paternal acres with his team,
    By mortgages unburdened, or by debt;
Who is not, like the soldier, by the bugle roused,
    Nor has to fear the raging of the sea;
Who keeps quite clear of " Change," and enters not
        the door
    Of proud and influential citizens.
And so he either weds the lofty poplar trees
    To the adult young offshoots of the vine;   10
Or keeps an eye upon his lowing herds, which graze
    In some sequestered glen among the hills;
Or trims away the barren branches with his shears,
    And grafts productive offsets in their room;
Or stores in well-rinsed wine-jars honey from the
        comb,
    Or shears the fleeces of his fly-baned ewes;
Or when old Autumn shows his honest head
        abroad

With crown of mellow apples on his hair,
Oh then how proud he feels in plucking grafted
        pears,
And grapes in purple clusters from the vine,   20
To offer them as gifts, Priapus, at thy shrine,
    And thine, Silvanus, guardian God of bounds.
He loves to lie at times beneath the old holm
        oak,
    Or sometimes on the velvet of the turf,
While, 'twixt their high banks, flow the waters of
        the brook,
    And sylvan warblers twitter in the shade ;
While from the gushing founts the bubbling wa-
        ters run,
    And challenge gentle slumbers by their tune.
But when the howling winter, dear to thundering
        Jove,
    Comes laden with its snowstorms and its 30
        showers,
He either beats the coverts with his baying pack,
    To drive the savage boars among his toils ;
Or on his slender poles sets net, with meshes fine,
    To trap the greedy thrushes on the lawn ;
Or snares the timid hare, may be, some roaming
        crane,
    And feels no little triumph in his feat.
Oh ! who would not forget amid such scenes as
        these
    The carking cares which anxious lovers feel ?

But if some virtuous matron take her proper charge
    Of cares domestic, and of infant loves,—   40
As doth the Sabine dame or ruddy sunburnt wife
    Who rules the sturdy boor's Apulian home ;—
And pile well-seasoned logs upon his sacred hearth
    What time her weary spouse is due at home ;
And drive the willing flock betwixt the wattled
    fence,
    And drain the milk from their distended dugs ;
And drawing jugs of home-made wine from out
    the cask,
    Provide impromptu feasts without a charge :
No Lucrine natives then would suit my taste so
    well,
    No royal dish to set before a king.—   50
If haply wild south-easters, thundering in the air,
    Should bring some finny dainties to our coast ;—
Nor would the Libyan sandgrouse please my palate
    more,
    Nor would Ionian quails me more delight
Than home-grown olives plucked from over-laden
    boughs,
    In my paternal grove of ancient trees,—
Than would the simple dish of homely sorrel-
    leaves,
    And wholesome mallows, good for invalids,—
Than would the lamb that is killed at boundary
    festivals,
    Than would the kid we rescued from the wolf. 60

K

Amidst such simple feasts how sweet it is to see
  The sheep led home from pasture to the fold :
To see the wearied oxen droop the languid neck,
  As home they drag the ploughshare upside down ;
And all the household-swarm that people well to do
  Are wont to gather round their groaning board.
In some such strain as this the usurer, Alpheus,
      spake ;—
  He always meant to lead a country life,
And so, called all his monies in upon the Ides,
  But, now the Kalends come, would put them 70
      out.

THE LEGEND OF THE SIBYLL.

A Free Translation from Ovid's Metamorphoses and the Æneid.

————*o*————

I 'WILL tell you a tale, if you'll listen,
 That Ovid once told with applause,
And who would affirm the old Romans
 Applauded without any cause?

It happened to Father Æneas
 That once, on his journey, he passed
The spot where his pilot, Misenus,
 A permanent anchor had cast.

So soon as the turrets of Naples
 Had faded away in his wake,—   10
Fair Naples, whose sorrowing minstrels
 Long wailed for Parthenope's sake,

He steered for the harbour of Cumæ,
 That marshy malarious shore,
Where once in her marvellous cavern
 The Sibyll resided of yore.

Deep down in the heart of the mountain
  Which springs from the edge of the lake,
Whose ominous name of Avernus
  Its waters will never forsake.   20

The mountain was dear to Apollo,
  The God who inspired her strain,
Among the grim crags on the summit
  He owned a magnificent fane.

Dim, gloomy, and vast was the cavern
  Where dwelt his high priestess below ;
In vain had men often been eager
  Its secret recesses to know.

It owned to a hundred windings,
  A hundred mouths did it own,   30
Whence rolled like the far-distant thunder
  The oracle's mystical moan.

Unveiling the womb of the future,
  The purport and aim of the past ;
Yet dealing in dubious phrases,
  Lest men should grow wise over fast.

So dread was the scene and the Priestess,
  Her votaries trembled with awe ;
Æneas ne'er paused at the portals,
  He quaked not for all that he saw.   40

He entered her cave, and besought her
　To grant him the wish of his heart,—
Permission to visit Avernus
　And talk with his father apart.

In silence she heard his petition,
　And fastened her eyes on the ground ;
His heart it beat loud till she raised them,
　And glanced with a wild look around.

The form of her visage was altered,
　And flushed was the hue of her face ;　50
Her long flowing tresses, dishevelled,
　She shook from their fillets apace.

Her stature grew more than a mortal's,
　Nor feminine now was her mien,
Her accents no longer they sounded
　At all like a woman's, I ween.

She felt the Divine inspiration,
　It maddened her under its yoke,
It coursed through her veins in its fury,
　It racked her full heart as she spoke.　60

" Oh, great is the boon that thou seekest,
　Unheard of, great hero," she said,
" But great is the fame of thy valour,
　Thy piety's fame is wide spread.

" Then be of good courage, O Trojan,
 The boon that thou seekest is thine !
Wouldst thou visit the regions of Orcus,
 The charge of thy journey be mine !

" I'll show thee the halls of Elysium,
 Thy parent—his face thou shalt see, 70
There's no path that may not be trodden
 When valour like thine is the plea."

She spoke, and revealed to his vision
 A bough that was gleaming with gold,
A bough that hung down in the forest
 Which Juno once owned, as I'm told.

She pointed it out, and then bade him
 Go pluck it in haste from the tree;
Æneas obeyed—in a moment
 His eyes were enabled to see 80

The wonders of terrible Orcus,
 Its ghostly mysterious glades,
The spirits of all his forefathers,
 The wealth and the ways of the shades.

He saw there his father Anchises,
 No longer weighed down by his years;
He learnt all the laws of his prison ;
 He told him his hopes and his fears :

He opened the books of the Parcæ,
  And mused on the mystical page ;　90
Learnt what were his hopes for the future,
  And what were the wars he should wage.

Till, weary at last, he bethought him,
  When little was left him to learn,
That back to the regions of daylight
  It might be as well to return.

Now, while he was slowly retracing
  His steps with the dame by his side,
He thought he would solace his journey
  By chatting awhile with his guide.　100

Iknow not," he said, " if thou really
  Art that which thy bearing implies,
A child of the gods, or a goddess,
  But such thou must rank in my eyes.

" I owe thee no small obligation,
  A sight of the regions of Death,
And safety amidst all the perils
  That threatened to cut off my breath.

" For this, thy fair favour, I'll promise
  So soon I return to the light,　110
I'll rear thee a shrine and a temple,
  And pay thee all honours aright ! "

The Prophetess heard his avowal,
  And heaved such a terrible sigh;
" I am not a Goddess," she answered;
  " Unworthy of incense am I.

" I will not attempt to mislead thee,
  My case it is sad, thou must know;
Thou wilt not refuse to believe me
  On hearing the tale of my woe.   120

" I once was beloved, and my suitor
  Was Phœbus himself, I declare;
He offered to make me immortal,
  If only his couch I would share.

" But while he was sighing and suing,
  And bribing me not to decline,
Said he: ' My fair damsel of Cumæ
  Whatever thou askest is thine !'

" I scooped up the sand, a good quantum,
  And showed him the handful I held,   130
And asked,—oh ! the foolish delusion,
  Doomed soon to be rued and dispelled—

" ' Oh grant me,' I said, ' great Apollo,
  So many long years to exist,
As granules of sand can be counted
  Among what I hold in my fist.'

" Alas for my thoughtless omission,
　　Alas, I forgot, to my ruth,
　To ask that my years of existence
　　Might bloom with perpetual youth.　　140

" Yet even this too he had granted,
　　He would not have grudged me the boon,
　Had I but agreed to his fancy,
　　And danced for a while to his tune.

" Alas, his fond suit I rejected,
　　And so I continue unwed—
　And years now sit heavily on me,
　　My youth and my beauty are fled.

" My steps, see they totter already,
　　My prospect o'erwhelms me with dread, 150
　The troubles of age are upon me,
　　I very much wish I were dead !

" Ten centuries I had petitioned,
　　But seven as yet have gone by,
　And still to complete the full number,
　　Three more must elapse ere I die.

" Three hundred more seasons of harvest,
　　Three hundred more seasons of spring ;
　Alas, what a terrible torment,
　　Oh, would that my soul could take wing ! 160

" It will not be long ere my body
    Will wholly be wasted away ;
I shall not have so much to carry,
    That much will be well, I dare say.

" None then will believe that I ever
    Could once have been dear to the god,
And Phœbus himself will deny it,
    And sanction his no with a nod.

" But tho' I shall be so much altered
    That none would my lineaments own,   170
My voice, it has never yet faltered,
    By that will the Sibyll be known."

Æneas, much moved with compassion,
    Expressed his regret at her choice ;
But long generations of Romans
    Remembered and honoured her voice.

THE EPILOGUE.

———o———

SONNET I.

THE DEATH.

As, when the baying hounds pick up the scent
　　Some royal stag hath left upon the leas,
　　And rouse him from the covert, where, at ease,
Among the brakes he lies, in calm content ;

And chase him up and down, till he is spent
　　With heat and toil, and courts the treacherous
　　　　breeze
　　Which fans his throbbing flanks and trembling
　　　　knees,
Or plunges in some pool, improvident,

Destined to die amongst the ravening pack,
　　Which rend him limb from limb, amidst the
　　　　brook ;
While horns ring out, and lashes loudly crack :

So when the cry of critics scent my book,
　　They 'will run it down, once they are on the track,
While I ring out its dirge, and take one last fond look.

SONNET II.

THE DIRGE.

The Master of the Forest and the stags
　　Is sometimes Master of the hounds as well;
　　He urges on the chase o'er flood and fell,
And feels no pang what time the quarry flags.

Why should he ?　Are there not beyond the crags
　　A hundred more that in his forest dwell
　　Who both in points and pace may yet excel ?
Then wherefore wince if one be torn to rags ?

He will not stay the chase, but take the horn,
　　And blow the blast himself; for in the fray
His brave stags will not all be overborne.

He knows full well that some will stand at bay,
　　And turn upon the hounds with scathing scorn ;
Then why should heart be faint, or spirit flag to-day ?

THE END.

Wyman & Sons, Printers, Great Queen Street, London, W.C.

www.ingramcontent.com/pod-product-compliance
Lightning Source LLC
Chambersburg PA
CBHW021121020726
47500CB00003B/861